I0726179

Two *Portraits* in Oil

E. Thornton Goode, Jr.

WORKBOOK PRESS LLC
187 E Warm Springs Rd,
Suite B285, Las Vegas, NV 89119, USA

Website: https://workbookpress.com/
Hotline: 1-888-818-4856
Email: admin@workbookpress.com

Ordering Information:
Quantity sales. Special discounts are available on quantity purchases by corporations, associations, and others.
For details, contact the publisher at the address above.

Library of Congress Control Number:

ISBN-13:   000-0-000000-00-0 (Paperback Version)
                000-0-000000-00-0 (Digital Version)

REV. DATE: 05/07/2022

Two Portraits in Oil

by

E. Thornton Goode, Jr.

In Dedication

I want to dedicate this novel to my good friend, Julian Green, who has been so kind to let me use his pictures in several of my novels and short stories. He is the likeness of several of my main characters. I wanted the reader to see his pictures to get an idea as to the appearance of those characters.

I cannot express how thankful I am he has allowed me to do this. In several of my novels, I make reference to a 'truly handsome man'. This is a man who is not only handsome on the outside but is handsome on the inside as well. Julian definitely fits the description.

Julian..… Many thanks, my Friend. Thank you for being in my life. I love you.

Thornton

My Julian went in for an operation on December 16, 2017. The operation was a success but he went into ane anesthesia coma. He was removed from the respirator and he passed away on Christmas Day, 2017. Julian, I miss you and will always love you.

All the king's horses and all the king's men will never put my heart back together again.

In Appreciation

I would like to thank my friend, Julian Green, for letting me use his picture, so the reader might get an idea as to the character of Farin in the story.

PROLOGUE

Dreams are an amazing thing. Most of the time, they are the brain letting off steam. I think that's why we can hardly remember them. Sometimes, they're more vivid and we do remember at least parts of them. Yes. There are many clinical explanations for dreams.

But there are some dreams that have other possible purposes. Some think they could be warnings or omens. Some believe past lives are tapping in. Others feel they are predictions of the future.

One largely held belief is it is one way for the dead to communicate with the living. George Anderson mentions this in his incredible book, <u>Lessons</u> <u>from</u> <u>the</u> <u>Light</u>.

I had a personal experience that was quite interesting. It involved my late first partner, Phillip. In the dream, I was looking at him and he was talking to me. In the background, I could see this older kid, bouncing around, doing cartwheels, yelling and screaming just having a terrific time.

Phillip looked at me. "This kid is about to wear me out. I was put in charge of him to make sure he doesn't hurt himself. The reason he's doing all this is because, when he was alive, he was in a wheelchair his entire life and couldn't talk or move. I'm not quite sure why I've been given charge of him but there has to be a reason."

Later, I found out from my late second partner, Dan, he had a younger brother, Marty, who had Cerebral Palsy and was in a wheelchair all his life. Marty died when he was like only twenty-one years old. The connection became perfectly clear to me.

There's been one reoccurring dream I've had for decades, going back to my teen years. Like every so many years, it would happen, so real and vivid. I'm in a stairwell, running up steps. At every landing, there's a long narrow window where I'm able to peer out. I'm trying to get as high as possible because I can look out and see a huge tidal wave coming. Was this dream a warning?

Of course, this dream was always funny as I was never living near the ocean. Throughout my whole life, I was hundreds of miles from the ocean. That is until I retired. Now, I live on the southwest coast of Mexico and the ocean is three hundred feet from the front door. Yeah. What can I say? Are you laughing or are you going "Oooooooo"?

In this story, the main character has a sequence of extremely realistic dreams which come to have a profound effect on his life. Also, he's unable to resist the urge to paint the portrait of an individual in his dreams.

Little did he realize the unbelievable meaning the painting and the dreams were going to have.

CHAPTER I

Riding my motorcycle into the parking lot, I parked, hit the kickstand with my foot, and shut off the motor. Without moving, I began to stare at the building. I'd never been there before in real life. But I was extremely familiar with it from my dreams. It was like déjà vu.

Bob told me I should come since my dreams had been so intense and realistic. So, here I sat just staring. I couldn't get over how every detail seemed to be there from my dreams. Suddenly, all the emotions and memories began to flood back into my head. Tears began to stream down my face, remembering all that had happened. I cried out. "I loved you so much." I shook my head. I had loved them both so much.

I knew I had to compose myself before going in. The tour guides would think me insane. Walking in, with tears running down my face, would definitely raise some concern on their part. I was sure. Then, it hit me. If I was this emotional in the parking lot, how would I feel when I walked through the door? Would everything become even greater and overwhelming? Maybe it would be best if I did not go in. Maybe I should just turn around and go back. But that would be ridiculous. For crying out loud, no pun intended, but I had to get a grip. They'd only been dreams. Just dreams.

I slowly took off my gloves and laid them on the handlebars. Then, I took off my helmet, holding it in my right hand. I looked up and stared at the building again. "Okay. Let's do this." I put my weight on my left foot, swung my right leg over the seat and stood firmly on the ground next to the bike. I grabbed my gloves, put them in my helmet, and stuck it on the backrest of the buddy seat.

Little did I realize. After a while, I'd be entering the premises and my entire life would be completely changed forever.

CHAPTER II

A short-order cook doesn't make that much. Money! Yeah. What can I say? It was two thousand fourteen and the beginning of May. I'd been saving for some time to take this upcoming vacation. Some of my paintings had sold and I'd received a few small royalty checks from my publisher from sales of the two books I had in print.

No, you won't find any of my paintings in fashionable galleries. Of course, I attribute it to not enough exposure. Grin! Believe it. Stop laughing.

As for my novels, you won't find them on the 'Best Seller' rack at your favorite bookstore, either. My novels aren't mainstream. You'll only find them in the 'alternative' section. My writing teacher said it was extremely important to write what you know. Well. I definitely know about the relationships between two men. What can I say? Now, you know why they are in the 'alternative' section. That's okay. I still have an audience for my works. My small royalty checks prove it.

With my education, some folks told me I should have chosen another profession where I could have made more money. But I really enjoyed being a short-order cook. It paid the bills and it afforded me flexible time. And believe it or not, sometimes there was money left over. I'm looking into doing some investing but I need to find someone who knows investing and finance.

I love the internet. It has allowed me to meet many people. Some are in foreign countries. Some are interesting enough that one day, I hope I might actually meet them in person. I was lucky enough several of those I'd met online invited me to stay with them while traveling, during my upcoming trip both on the way up and back again.

This was going to be an amazing trip. A month-long outing to the upper coast of New England to paint. Why New England? It was time to get away from doing landscapes and still life paintings. I wanted to try my hand at painting the ocean.

*   *   *   *   *

Yes. I believe the ocean is one of the most difficult things to paint. I've always admired those who have the ability to capture it on canvas and make it look real.

There's one other thing that's very difficult to paint. Portraits. Every person is a singular being with his own physical characteristics. If you're off the slightest in trying to capture that person, it is no longer him. Oh. It'll look similar to him but everyone who sees the painting will know it's a little 'off'.

For this reason, I've steered away from painting portraits and seascapes. Landscape and still life subjects are simple. You paint a tree, everyone knows it's a tree. You paint a mountain and everyone knows it's a mountain. It's the same with apples, grapes and wine glasses.

I have heard people say. "Oh. I'll never be able to paint." Well, they have two problems. One is described so well in a quote from the book, Illusions, by Richard Bach. 'Quote your limitations and sure enough, they're yours.' I think it's quite self-explanatory. The other problem is they haven't learned to see. They see but they really don't SEE.

A perfect example of this was the time I was asked to take a few folks and guide them painting. Maybe give them a few pointers. So, we all set up easels in the room and I told them to paint me the sky with clouds, a tree, and some grass from their imagination and memory. Maybe put a mountain in the background. It was a test. Well, everyone got out their tubes of blue, white, brown and green paint. Onto the canvases went the blue for the sky, white for the clouds, brown for the tree trunk and green for the leaves and grass. After a little while, I began to hear snickering and chuckles.

"What's the matter?" I asked knowingly.

One chimed in. "Something's wrong. They don't look right. They don't look real. Everything's so flat."

"Oh, really? And why is that?" Came my smiling response.

"I don't know."

"Well. I'm going to tell you why. It's because you can't see." A questioning expression filled all their faces. "That's right. You assume. You don't see. Is the sky blue? Is a cloud white? Is a tree brown and green? NO! But you think they are. Even after seeing them your entire lives, you think they are. You haven't learned to really see them. Now. We're going outside and we're going to look at several things. Let's go."

So, we marched outside and began to look.

I pointed straight up. "What color is the background sky?"

"It's a blue." One answered.

Then, I pointed at the sky at the horizon. "What color is the sky over there?"

"Oh, my God. It's a hazy lighter blue." They spoke in amazement.

"Now. Look at the color gradation from the blue above us to the hazy sky on the horizon."

Everyone bent their heads to see.

"And look at the clouds. They have all sorts of grays and blues and yellows mixed in with the whites. Yes?"

"Geez. He's right."

"Okay. Now, look at the hills nearest us and then at the ones in the far distance." I paused. "Do you see the difference? Okay. We all know the same trees and rocks make up all those hills. Why is there a difference? Why do the ones in the distance look bluer and grayer and less defined?"

"Oh. Wow. I see!"

"THAT is called atmospheric perspective. The moisture and dust in the air distort the light and gives a haze to distant objects. Now. Are you beginning to see?"

It was the same with the trees and grass and everything. Shades and shadowing change the light on everything. Finally, they were beginning to see it.

Needless to say, when they started painting again before they painted the clouds, they went to the window and really looked at the clouds in the sky to see the different colors and shading. They had begun to see and their paintings proved it. They would NEVER look at anything the same way again.

One even smiled and looked up after finishing his painting. "Damn. Maybe I can paint after all."

I smiled. He had accomplished the last important element. He had removed the stumbling block of his limitations.

*   *   *   *   *

I'd planned this trip for months, making sure they had backup at work while I was gone. There were several online guys I chatted with who lived along the route I was taking. I wanted to make sure it would be okay to spend the night. Bob, who lived in Portland, Maine, told me I could spend the whole month with him if I wanted.

The week before leaving, I began organizing the things I wanted to take with me. Of course, I wanted to take my paints, brushes, and fold-up easel. Canvases, linseed oil, and turpentine would be available in an art shop in Portland. I also chose my clothes very carefully. Since it was summer, I'd be wearing shorts most of the time, short sleeve shirts, and T-shirts. I did set aside a nice pair of jeans and long sleeve shirt in case I went out one evening. When riding, I'd always be wearing jeans, a shirt, jacket, boots, and gloves. They were for some protection in the event something happened. If you know what I mean. I also had to bring a few baseball caps since I'd be outdoors in the sun. If you're bald like me, you totally understand what I'm talking about.

After arranging everything carefully, I was pretty sure I could get all the items I wanted to bring with me on my bike. Okay. I hear you laughing. But trust me. You'd be surprised how much you can get on a thirteen hundred, cruiser-style motorcycle with saddlebags, a luggage rack, and a buddy seat with backrest. Even my seat had a backrest. You have no idea how comfortable it is to ride, leaning back with your feet up on the roll bars. Yep. So comfortable, you could almost fall asleep. Almost.

It was several days before I left when the dreams started. These weren't just regular dreams. They were so intense, that during waking hours, I could remember every detail. The first of the dreams was a recollection. A flashback in time. It was how it all began.

* * * * *

My family was quite well-to-do. One of the old established families of Boston. We knew all the notable and important families. I remember. I never wanted for anything. That's how well-off we were. It was doubtful I'd ever have to work during my lifetime if I didn't want to.

I was eighteen and about ready to go off to study at the Art Academy later in the year. Over time, my parents had seen my inclination for art. My main interest was in oils. For a few years, my mother had been talking about me with a lady of one of the Boston families. The lady was an artist and had seen some of my work. Her son was becoming quite well known in the art world.

She thought it would be extremely beneficial to my art career if I studied with him. So, upon graduation from high school, my parents arranged for me to go and apprentice with her son.

Her son had left New York City and decided to take up residence in Prouts Neck, Maine. He wanted to paint more oceanscapes. In the beginning, I'd not only go up and apprentice with him in art but I'd also help him set up his Studio. This was a carriage house, being converted. The renovations would still be in progress while I was there, during the first visit. Because of our age difference, him being forty-seven, I would call him Uncle. It was settled.

When I arrived, there were several people waiting on the platform for folks to get off the train. I wasn't sure which one was Uncle Winslow. But as I stepped off the train, I saw a man, heading in my direction.

I'm not really sure what I'd expected. But here came a man who was virtually my same height and build. Just older. Maybe it's because, in my mind, I imagined all great and wonderful artists being tall and imposing figures.

I'd brought with me a good supply of paints, brushes, canvases, sketchbooks, and the like. Uncle Winslow was very helpful, getting me and my things in the wagon. Then, we left the station.

After a while, I tried to make small talk. "I'm really looking forward to this time with you. I believe I'll be able to learn quite a bit."

His response had almost an uncaring tone. "Good."

It was then, I realized the rest of the trip would be done in silence.

When we arrived at the Studio, he helped me get situated in a little side room. For the first few days, I helped him arrange things the way he wanted, trying to stay out of the workers' way. A Mr. John Stevens and his crew were the ones renovating the place. He was Uncle Winslow's architect.

Over the next few days, we took several trips out to look at the ocean. Both of us made several rough sketches we could use later. While out observing, Uncle Winslow wasn't very talkative. Once back at the Studio, Uncle Winslow would set up a canvas, get out his paints and begin a picture. I set mine up next to his, so I might watch him as I painted. To me, it was amazing to watch him applying paint to the canvas. The images seemed to appear almost magically and so lifelike. It was as if his mind had captured the instantaneous moment a wave had crashed onto one of the rocks and the image was reappearing on the canvas.

I, too, was applying paint to my canvas. Desperately, I tried to make it look real and lifelike but alas. I remember Uncle Winslow, turning his head, looking over at my canvas. His face slightly grimaced and he let out a low grunt. Then, reaching over with his brush, he placed several strokes of paint upon the waves I was painting. Instantly, the waves became more real. My mouth opened wide and I let out a sigh of happiness. I turned and looked at him, smiling. A huge grin of satisfaction filled his face.

The next day, we went out again with our sketchbooks. We sat on some rocks to watch the ocean. I noticed Uncle Winslow doing a sketch.

I looked hard at the ocean and watched it very carefully. With my pencil, I started drawing wave formations but making particular note of the smaller details. I also noted the color variations in a wave due to the sunlight passing through it. I even drew arrows to certain spots to label a specific color.

Out of the corner of my eye, I saw Uncle Winslow had turned his head slightly, saw what I was doing and his mouth formed a grin. He spoke quietly. "Well. You're beginning to really see. Excellent."

We must have sat there for at least three hours and he never said another word. Finally, I saw him close his sketchbook. It was time to head back.

On the way back to the Studio, we went down to where the fishermen were to see about maybe getting fish for dinner. That's when I saw those incredible eyes. Blue as a deep lagoon.

He was just over six feet tall and looked to be in his early twenties. He was standing with a group of other fishermen who were in their late thirties and early forties. The subject of conversation seemed to be about the catch of the day. He seemed to be listening and not entering the discussion.

Uncle Winslow and I just quietly passed by, not saying a word.

I couldn't help myself. Momentarily, I stopped, glancing in HIS direction. I saw his head turn and his eyes looked directly into mine. I was so jolted, totally captured by his amazing blue eyes. It was like he could see my soul. Then, he smiled.

Suddenly, I realized Uncle Winslow was somewhat ahead of me. I quickly turned away and never looked back. But there was more. At that moment, I felt something. It was like something, gripping my body. I felt a connection with him. Uncle Winslow was teaching me well. Every detail of his clean-shaven face, wavy hair the color of dark chocolate, and those intense, ice blue eyes were embedded in my brain. Quickly, I caught up to Uncle Winslow as we headed home.

That night as I lay in bed, thinking about the young fisherman, it drove me crazy. I couldn't stop thinking about him.

CHAPTER III

The next day at work, there came a lull in business. Joe, one of the waiters, and I sat down to have a cup of coffee.

Joe looked at me and smiled. "Just a few more days and you'll be off on your vacation. I know you can't wait. That's a pretty long haul on a bike, isn't it?"

"Yeah. But my bike is so comfortable. You can lean back and almost fall asleep, it's so comfortable. I try not to do more than three hundred miles a day. Normally, four hundred at the max. That's almost a ten-hour day on the expressway. But there are exceptions." I smiled. "The first leg of this trip is almost six hundred miles. Yeah. THIS is one of the exceptions. If I really haul ass at around seventy to seventy-five miles an hour, I can do it in about the same amount of time. Maybe a little longer. Yeah. I haven't seen Michael since school, so I may ask him if I can stay over another day to really get rested up."

"You said something about Portland, Maine. Why there?" Joe twitched his head. "How far is that?"

"It's about thirteen hundred maybe fourteen hundred miles. But it's expressway all the way. What can I say? That area of the country is great for painting the ocean. One of America's greatest seascape artists lived up in that area. Winslow Homer." I drew a deep gasp. "Oh, my God! Winslow Homer."

Joe looked at me strangely. "What's wrong with Winslow Homer?"

I looked off into space and spoke quietly. "Winslow Homer. Could it be? He's Uncle Winslow?"

There was a questioning expression on Joe's face. "Uncle Winslow?"

I looked right at Joe. "I had the strangest dream last night. Never had a dream like it before. I can tell you in detail the entire dream. It was that real."

Joe shook his head. "Uncle Winslow?"

"I was some eighteen-year-old rich kid from Boston who went to study with an artist who happened to be the son of a friend of my mother. Because of our age difference, even though not a relative, they said I should call him 'uncle'."

Joe chuckled. "And this was your Uncle Winslow?"

"Yeah. He was setting up a painting studio in a place called Prouts Neck, Maine. It was going to be his first year there. The plan was I'd go and apprenticed with him for a month. Maybe a little longer. And also help him set up his Studio. Every summer after that while studying at the Art Academy, I'd go up for a month or more and study with Uncle Winslow. In the dream I had last night, I'd only been there for maybe two weeks."

Joe snickered. "Just a sec." He pulled out his iPad and started typing. He began to mumble. "Winslow… Homer… Studio… Prouts… Neck… Maine." He paused and kept looking at the screen. "Does this look like it might be the place?" He turned the screen of his iPad toward me.

I gasped. "Holy crap! That's it! Well, they're still working on it. Renovating it from a carriage house into his living quarters. But, yeah. That's it!"

Joe pulled the iPad back. "Just for your information, Prouts Neck is just south of Portland. Thought you might like to know." He looked squarely at me. "You do realize we're talking about eighteen eighty-three here. That's when Winslow Homer moved to Maine and remained there for the rest of his life." He then typed. "Winslow… Homer." He kept staring at the screen. Then a big smile filled his face. "Could this possibly be your Uncle Winslow?" He turned the iPad in my direction.

"Oh, my God! That's him! That's Uncle Winslow!" I shook my head. "Eighteen eighty-three! Now, things are beginning to make a little sense. But why was my dream so intense?"

Joe smiled. "Dreams are strange things. I've always believed certain dreams are premonitions or warnings. Not all dreams. But sometimes, we all have those weird, unexplainable, unforgettable dreams. I also believe dreams are ways for the dead to communicate with us. So, who knows?" Joe chuckled and gave me a weird exotic look. "Maybe you're on your way to meet your Destiny." He bent his head down and started to laugh. "Seriously. I'd love to hear more about this." Then, he got serious again. "Hey. You're a writer. You need to write all this stuff down. It might be your next novel."

"Damn. You know? You're right. I'll get this on the computer ASAP."

"So, that's all you remember?" Joe questioned again.

"Well. What I told you is really about it. Except..." I stared off into space and smiled.

Joe sat up straight. "Okay! Okay! 'Enquiring minds want to know.' There is more. Out with it." He started laughing.

I bent my head down. "There was this guy. This fisherman. If only you could have seen his eyes. Like the ice of a blue berg."

A huge grin filled Joe's face. "Wow. Maybe there really IS more to this."

I looked right at Joe. "Joe. In the dream, I was eighteen. I'm thirty-six right now. A huge difference in age." I paused for a moment and smiled. "But he was so damned incredibly handsome. Early twenties, dark brown hair. And I swear to God there was this incredible instantaneous connection."

"What!" Joe blurted out. "Ah! Excuse me! I heard nothing of fur on the face. You always go for these guys with furry faces."

"Yeah. I know. But this guy was so good-looking. Square jawline. What can I say?"

We both laughed.

When I went to bed that night, the dream returned. It seemed to continue where the previous night's dream ended.

*   *   *   *   *

As the days went by, Uncle Winslow began to mellow. He became more communicative. I believe it's because he finally realized I wasn't just some snot-nosed, little, rich kid mommy and daddy wanted to get out of their hair for the summer. He saw I was listening. He saw I was paying attention. He saw I was seeing and applying all of it on canvas.

We returned one afternoon to the Studio after doing some sketching when Uncle Winslow looked at me and smiled. "There's something I wanted to mention. It happened a little over a week ago at the dock. I wanted you to know. I saw what happened."

I looked at him with a questioning expression. "What?"

"You. Looking at that fisherman boy." He smiled.

"Well. I. Well." I was so flustered I didn't know what to say. He was constantly in my thoughts. I hung my head down.

Uncle Winslow looked at me and smiled. "Sit down, my boy. I want to explain something to you. Whether you know it or not, you are different. And there's nothing wrong with it. Don't ever let anyone tell you there's something wrong with it. You're eighteen and beginning to understand certain things. But the way your mind works is different from the ways of other men. Now. You must understand you're not alone. There are others who think and feel the same way and have the same mindset you do. But. You must be very careful. The way you think and understand is not accepted by most people. Remember that. Just be careful."

He paused for a moment then continued. "I did notice. He looked back. And smiled." He smiled. "And I must say. He's a very good-looking young man." A big grin filled his face. "We'll talk more of this at another time."

I knew what he was talking about. Uncle Winslow was right. I could feel it inside me. Things I'd been wondering about myself were becoming perfectly crystal clear.

During the rest of the time I spent at the Studio, I never saw the handsome fisherman again. I attributed it to the possible time we went down to the docks. He may have gone home or was still out fishing.

I accomplished completing two canvases. Uncle Winslow indicated I shouldn't be ashamed of them. He thought they were very good.

The last conversation we had was before I left.

Uncle Winslow smiled. "In the beginning, I wasn't really sure how this was going to work out. But I have enjoyed our time together. I see you're a fast learner. I look forward to next year."

As unusual and strange as Uncle Winslow was, I, too, was looking forward to the next year's session with him. I remember. I was smiling as I waved to him while the train pulled away from the station. He, too, was smiling as he waved.

*　*　*　*　*

I got up early, turned on the computer and went into my dictation program. In no time at all, I had notations, time sequences, descriptions, and comments to make me remember everything. That way down the road, I could fill in and write the more fluid and complex story.

The minute I arrived at work the next day, Joe came running up to me. "You dreamed last night? Tell me. What happened? Did you see your fisherman again?"

I laughed. "Yes. The dream continued last night. But there was nothing of the fisherman."

Joe punched his right fist into his left palm. "Damn! And I was so hoping."

We both broke out laughing.

"I will tell you. I have taken your advice. I've made notes and comments. They're on my computer."

Joe smiled. "Good. And make sure you back everything up on a thumb drive in case something should happen to the damn computer."

I laughed. "I'm way ahead of you on that. I do that with all my writing projects. Just in case. Yeah."

That night I slept like a rock. I don't remember dreaming anything. But the next night was different. It began with me already at the Studio.

*   *   *   *   *

I was sitting next to Uncle Winslow with my left arm over his shoulder. We were slowly rocking from side to side. Uncle Winslow was sobbing. I was speaking quietly. "I was so sorry to hear about your mother. She was an amazing lady. If not for her, I'd never have met you. I'm so, so sorry."

Uncle Winslow's mother had passed away that April. He was extremely distraught. Many thought I shouldn't come but I thought differently. I knew if I had lost my mother, I would have liked to have had someone there to comfort me. I patted his right knee with my right hand.

With his left hand, he took my right hand in his and slightly squeezed. "Thank you. Thank you so much for coming. I truly appreciate it."

It was the summer of eighteen eighty-four and I knew it was going to be a rather somber stay. Uncle Winslow was having a tendency to sleep later than normal. So, I'd get up and fix coffee in the fireplace and cook some eggs and bacon in an iron skillet. They were kept in the ice chest out on the porch. The skillet and coffee pot rested on an iron grill over the fire in the fireplace. When ready, I'd go roust him out of bed. "Rise and shine, sleepyhead. A day of painting awaits." I'd start to chuckle.

"Oh. Do I have to get up? I don't really want to get up." He'd call from under the covers.

"Oh, yes! Breakfast is ready! Time to get this show on the road!" I tugged at the covers.

"Okay! Okay! I'm up! Go pour the coffee!" He started to

laugh.

I stayed with Uncle Winslow for much more than a month to make sure his grieving had finally crested. During that time period, we did work on a few canvases but a lot of the time was spent just talking. I let him tell me about his life so far as well as the influence his mother had on his artistic ability. I'd seen several of her excellent watercolors.

*　*　*　*　*

Watercolor is not an easy medium. It is totally unforgiving. Unlike oils where if you make a mistake, you can take a palette knife, scrape it off and do it again.

*　*　*　*　*

The whole time I was there that summer, I never saw the handsome fisherman. Maybe it was for the best. But I still couldn't get him out of my mind.

Before getting on the train, Uncle Winslow gave me a big hug. "My boy. Thank you so much for coming. It was a tremendous help to me. I gratefully appreciated it."

As I got on the train, I waved my goodbye and smiled. Uncle Winslow was better. He waved and smiled back at me.

CHAPTER IV

When I arrived at work, we were very busy. Joe called out. "At break, I want to hear if there's anything new to tell." He started to laugh.

I just turned, looked at him and gave him a silent grin.

When break time arrived, we grabbed our cups of coffee and quickly sat down. Since we were so busy, we were going to cut our break short.

"The dream last night was rather sad. Uncle Winslow's mother had died. He was very upset when I'd arrived but was much better by the time I left." I looked right at Joe. "And no. There was no sign of my fisherman. Maybe he was just a passing fantasy in the dream."

Joe looked disappointed. "Oh, well. That's too bad. I had great hopes." He paused for a moment and smiled. "But those dreams aren't over yet. And he's still out there in your dream somewhere."

"You think so? Well, we shall see." I grinned.

As my shift ended, Joe came up to me and smiled. "Try and get some good rest tonight. You have a long road ahead of you tomorrow. Take it easy. I don't want to hear about you on the six o'clock news." He smiled and gave me a big hug. "And when you get back, I want to hear the rest of the dreams. Yeah. I know there's more to come. I just know it."

Getting home that evening, I snugly packed the saddlebags with art supplies and locked them. I packed my small satchel with smaller items and my computer. It would go into the large carryall along with clothes and other items then be stretched over the buddy seat with the ends, resting on top of the saddlebags. My fold-up easel would go on top of the carryall. The camera case would go on the back luggage rack. With everything in readiness, I went to bed. I wasn't surprised when the dream returned.

*   *   *   *   *

I was twenty-four and my six years of education at the Art Academy had ended. My professors were extremely pleased with my work and told me I was a very, very good artist. Little did they realize. I owed all I really knew to Uncle Winslow. This summer was going to be the last one I would spend with him. Knowing this, we spent a significant time in conversation. Yes. We did paint. I did one canvas. Uncle Winslow was extremely pleased with it. Since all my other previous canvases had been shipped to my parents in Boston after they were dry, I wanted to leave this one for Uncle Winslow as a token of my appreciation for all he'd done for me.

Again, there had been no sign of the fisherman. I could not help it but he continued to linger in my mind.

*   *   *   *   *

The next morning, I got up very early. Dawn was just around the corner in about two hours. I taped the wooden shaft of my rainbow flag to the backrest of the buddy seat then packed everything as planned on the bike, strapped it all down with bungee cords to make sure all was balanced and secure and I was off. A quick stop was made the night before at the nearby gas station to make sure my tank was full. Yep! My vacation had begun. Next stop, Richmond!

Riding the expressways made it easy to travel at seventy-plus miles an hour. Got up to speed, put on the throttle lock, my feet up on the roll bars, leaned back, and relaxed. I'd be stopping every hundred and fifty to a hundred and seventy-five miles for gasoline and maybe to eat something if I was hungry.

From Atlanta to Richmond and my buddy Mike's house, was about five hundred and seventy-five miles. I was giving myself eleven to twelve hours to get there. Starting around four in the morning to avoid early traffic in Atlanta, I hoped to be in Richmond by late afternoon. If there were any problems along the way, I'd call Mike on my cell phone.

If you've ever ridden a motorcycle on the open road, you realize there's a lot of time for you to ponder and think. Yes, I was enjoying the scenery and the countryside but my mind kept dwelling on my recent intense dreams. I also kept thinking of what Joe had said. Could there be some meaning in them?

Since I wasn't normally a speed demon on the highway, I'd travel in the right-hand lane. Seventy-plus miles an hour was fast enough for me. Many cars passed me, honking their horns, smiling, and giving me a 'thumbs-up'. They'd point to the back of my bike. They were referring to the rainbow flag. I'd turn my head to the left, shake it in the affirmative and give them a 'thumbs-up' in thanks with my left hand.

Racing up the road, I was finally crossing the border from Georgia into North Carolina. There was Charlotte, Raleigh and into Virginia. Hopewell, Petersburg, and finally, reaching Richmond. I was correct. It was going on four o'clock when I reached Michael's. He wanted me to park my bike in his garage, so I wouldn't have to unload it. I could get what I needed and leave the rest.

He was correct. I'd packed the large carryall, so I could unzip it and pull out my smaller satchel with my computer and all that goes with it as well as my toiletries.

It was good to see him. We hadn't seen each other since school. There were several pictures and videos I took with my cameras. Mike wanted one of him on my bike before I parked it for the night in the garage.

We sat up very late, talking. There was a lot we had to catch up on. It was great fun and the cocktails kept the conversation going. Michael had taken the next day off in hopes I'd stay over. I was glad. I was in no hurry and on no time schedule. I thought it was a great idea, so I could rest after that long ride.

It was late and we knew we had to go to bed. Do you know how it is when you have to sleep in a bed, not your own? Well, strangely enough, the bed at Michael's house was extremely comfortable. I fell asleep immediately. And, yes. I began to dream.

*　*　*　*　*

I realized I was thirty-six, in New York City and writing a letter to Uncle Winslow. Yes, even at thirty-six, I was still calling him Uncle Winslow. For now, he was sixty-five.

Dear Uncle Winslow,

I know it has been twelve long years since I have seen or contacted you. Of that, I am sincerely sorry. The last time I saw you I was twenty-four. It seems like a thousand years ago. I have thought about you, so many times since then and hoped you were well. Because of your tutoring and training, I got a very good job after graduating from the Art Academy.

The reason I am contacting you is that I have a request. I was wondering if I could come for a lengthy visit. There are many things turning over in my head and I would like very much to be able to discuss them with you. If you think my visit would not be a good idea, I would totally understand.

I would very much like to see what you have been working on recently and maybe do a canvas or two myself.

Let me know at your earliest convenience. It would be gratefully appreciated.

Your humble and respectful student.

Richie

I was smiling as I folded the letter and placed it in the envelope. I truly hoped I'd be able to make the visit.

It was strange but it all still seemed very logical just as all things seem logical in a dream. I was now, getting up from my seat on a train and heading for the door. Before stepping down, I looked out, and there on the platform with a big smile on his face was Uncle Winslow. Instantly, there was joy and happiness in my heart. I looked directly at him and smiled. I called out. "Uncle Winslow! So good to see you!"

"Richie! My boy! It's good to see you as well. How have you been? You look so handsome with your beard and mustache."

I lifted my hat to show my bald head and I gave a crazy smile.

Uncle Winslow laughed and pointed. "Grass does not grow on a busy street." He continued to laugh.

I ran over to him, set my satchel down and gave him a big hug. A huge feeling of comfort and joy came over me. My mind began to wonder why it had taken me so long to request this reunion.

We gathered all of my luggage, placing it in the wagon and we were off to the Studio.

Finally arriving, we moved all my things into the little room. I immediately went into my luggage and pull out the box I had packed with several items I'd brought for Uncle Winslow. Picking it up, I went into the studio room. "Uncle Winslow. I brought you a few things from New York I thought you could use." I set the box down on the table.

Uncle Winslow came over. "For me? And what do we have here?" He opened the box. "Oh, my boy. You're a godsend. Just look. Brushes, paints, and palette knives. Thank you. Thank you, my boy." He walked over and hugged me tightly.

I smiled. "It's one way I wanted to thank you for letting me come to visit."

Uncle Winslow smiled. "Thank you, my boy. I do appreciate it. Paints are getting so expensive these days." He chuckled.

"Tonight, we go to celebrate at your favorite restaurant. That one in the hotel. There's no way we're going to cook in the fireplace tonight."

After getting cleaned up and organized, we got in the wagon and headed to the hotel.

The restaurant wasn't very crowded and the waiter showed us immediately to a table. Before sitting down, I turned to the waiter. "Thank you so very much. This is a very important and special occasion. I haven't seen my Uncle Winslow in twelve years. Please, don't feel rushed, regarding anything. Take your time. We are in no hurry. And the night is on me."

The waiter smiled and bowed his head slightly. "No problem, Sir. We will take excellent care of you. If you need anything, my name is David." He looked at Uncle Winslow. "It is truly an honor to see you again and to serve the great Mr. Homer tonight. Please, don't hesitate if you need anything."

I extended my hand and shook his. "Thank you, David." When I sat down and placed my hat in the nearby chair, I looked at Uncle Winslow. "I want you to order whatever you want. The sky's the limit. I've done well because of you." I gave him a big smile.

Uncle Winslow smiled and bowed his head slightly. "Thank you, my boy. Thank you."

David smiled and slightly bowed. "Please. If you need anything, don't hesitate to let me know." He left the table.

As we began to get comfortable, I started to peruse the restaurant to see the other patrons. I could see in all directions except behind me.

Sitting across from me, Uncle Winslow could see where I couldn't. He leaned slightly forward. "There's a man over there, sitting alone across the room. He's looking in this direction. I saw him when we came in and he watched us the total time we walked to this table."

I was surprised. "Really? I wonder what that could be about?"

Uncle Winslow started to chuckle. "Well. I have a feeling we're getting ready to find out. He just got up and is headed this way."

I shifted quickly in my chair to look in the man's direction. He had very dark brown hair, beard and mustache and was looking directly at me. That's when I saw them. He had incredible blue eyes, looking directly into mine.

I was so stunned, I couldn't move or stop staring at him. I slowly whispered. "Oh, my God. It's him. I know it's him."

As he walked toward us even in clothes, I could tell he was much more muscular than he was eighteen years earlier. He was such an incredibly, handsome man. Within seconds, he was standing by the table. I quickly stood up and looked into his face.

He looked down into mine and smiled. With a deep resounding voice, he spoke. "I hope you don't mind me interrupting but I have to find out. I believe I know you. It's been a very long time. But somehow, I know you." He tilted his head slightly to the side.

I smiled and extended my hand. "Yes. I think we did meet. Sort of. Not formally. It was down at the fishing docks some eighteen years ago."

He took my hand, shaking it. A huge smile filled his face. "It is you. Boo. I knew it was you." He shook his head and bent it down in slight embarrassment. "Oh. I'm sorry. I call you, Boo.

I gave you that named after I first saw you. It's a long story. You might think it silly." He bent his head down again.

I smiled and spoke with excitement. "Then, please. Call me Boo. I like it. By the way, this is my Uncle Winslow. We are celebrating. Please. Please, come join us. You seem to be alone. Please." I gestured to the empty seat to my right.

He smiled. "I would like that as long as I'm not intruding."

Uncle Winslow had stood up and smiled. "Not at all, young man. Please."

He extended his hand toward Uncle Winslow. "Farin. Farin Harrington. Nice to finally meet you, Mr. Homer."

Uncle Winslow extended his hand and shook Farin's. "Nice to meet you, Farin. Please. Please, join us."

Farin turned and raised his right hand in the air to get the attention of the waiter. The waiter looked over and totally understood the situation. He smiled and shook his head in the affirmative. Farin smiled.

We all sat down. The waiter immediately placed a setting of flatware, plates and glasses in front of Farin. "I'll get your drink from your table, Mr. Harrington."

Farin looked at the waiter and smiled. "Thank you, David."

The waiter smiled. "My pleasure, Sir." He looked at us. "Might I get you something before you order?"

Uncle Winslow and I made our drink order as David handed out menus. There wasn't a great selection but it didn't matter. It was the company and conversation that was important. We quickly perused the menu and ordered.

"Thank you, gentlemen. I'll have your drinks in a minute. Mr. Harrington, I'll get you another." David left the table.

Farin looked at me and smiled. "I saw you come in and even with your beard and mustache, I just knew it was you. Don't ask me how. I just did. Boo. It's really you." He chuckled. "I see your hair has moved from the top of your head to your face."

We all laughed.

Uncle Winslow snickered. "I told him grass does not grow on a busy street."

We all continued to laugh.

I smiled. "Farin. You, too. You now have facial hair and it's extremely becoming on you. It looks like you've been doing some working out as well." I grinned.

Farin bent his head down and chuckled. "It's all that hauling in of the fish. You'd be surprised the workout it gives you. But I don't get out that much anymore. My uncles and cousins are doing most of the business lately. I stick around and do the bookkeeping." He laughed.

Just then, David arrived with our drinks. "If you need a refill, just let me know." He smiled and bowed his head slightly then moved away.

Farin turned to Uncle Winslow. "Sir. It is a privilege and an honor to finally meet you. I haven't been fortunate enough to see your work but I've heard people talk. They say you're the foremost seascape artist in the country. Maybe the world."

Uncle Winslow chuckled. "My boy. You are very kind. You must come by the Studio and see what I... we are working on. I have one finished and one almost complete, sitting on the easel right now."

Farin smiled and his eyes sparkled. "I'd very much like that. Yes, I would."

Uncle Winslow spoke again. "We're there most of the time. Come by tomorrow if you like. Come in the morning and we can have coffee and show you around."

Farin smiled. "Excellent. Excellent." Then he turned to me. "So. Where have you been all this time? I saw you that day. You looked to still be in school. Since both you and Mr. Homer were carrying sketchbooks, I took it you were studying with him. How lucky you are to have been able to study with such a well-known artist." He paused for a moment. "But I never saw you again. I heard you'd come for a month or so every summer after that but I never saw you. Probably with me being out fishing or at the lighthouse, I missed seeing you."

I questioned. "The lighthouse?"

"Yes. I'd sometimes go up and help out at the Cape Elizabeth Lighthouse. I got to know its workings and everything, so even now, I sometimes go up and help out."

"Oh. Wow! A lighthouse."

"If you're here long enough, I'll have to take you up there and show it to you." He smiled. "Now, what have you been doing all this time?"

"Well, after I graduated from the Art Academy, my last visit here was when I was twenty-four. That was twelve years ago. That's when I went to New York to work. I got an excellent job when they realized I had apprenticed with Uncle Winslow. And it pays very well, too. So, keep your wallet in your pocket. Tonight is on me."

We all laughed, raised our glasses up, clinking them together. "Hear! Hear!" We called together in our laughter.

Farin looked at me and smiled. "Thank you, Boo. I truly appreciate your kindness."

CHAPTER V

I awoke with a big smile on my face. "Farin. His name is Farin. And he calls me Boo. I wonder why? Interesting. And my name then was Richie."

I got up, dressed and went to the kitchen where Michael was gearing up to cook.

Michael looked up from his cutting. "I thought you were going to sleep a lot longer. But it's okay. We're going to have a relaxing day here just sitting, talking and cocktailing." He started laughing.

I joined in the laughter.

"Well, I hope you slept well."

I shook my head. "I did. But."

"But? What but? Is the bed not comfortable?" He looked at me with a distressed expression.

"Oh. No. No. The bed is wonderful. It's the dream. It's continuing." I smiled. "I never mentioned it last night. We were catching up on our lives since school."

"A dream. Okay. This sounds interesting. And it's continuing? What does that mean?"

"It started a little over a week ago. This dream. So real, I remember every detail. And it continues. Each time I dream, it picks up where the last one ended."

Mike's face scrunched up. "Now, that is really weird. You being a writer, I hope you're writing all of this stuff down. It sounds quite unusual."

I laughed. "Funny you should say that. I have my computer with me and I've been dictating notes, so I can remember everything."

Mike shook his head, laughing. "I swear. You writers get your inspiration from the strangest places. Why wouldn't dreams be one of the sources?"

I chuckled. "You've got that right."

"All right. You have my curiosity up. I want to hear this." Mike paused for a moment. "Is it over yet?"

"I don't think so. I have a feeling there's a lot more to it."

"Okay. After we eat, we're going to sit down, relax and I want to hear everything so far. One question. Please, tell me there is an interesting man in the dreams."

I bent down laughing hard. "Actually, there are TWO very interesting men in this dream sequence and one of them, believe it or not, is Winslow Homer."

"What!? Winslow Homer? The artist, Winslow Homer?"

"Yep. The one and only."

"I don't care how early it is. This definitely calls for a Bloody Mary. Hey! As Jimmy Buffett and Alan Jackson sing it. 'It's five o'clock somewhere.'"

We both roared with laughter.

As we sat chilling out and drinking our Bloody Marys, I began telling Michael the dreams. I wondered if he might have some insight into them.

After a while, Mike interrupted me. "Question. I'm curious. Does any of this have any validity? Yeah. I know they're dreams. Is it possible due to their intensity, there's some validity to them?"

I shook my head. "I doubt it. I think my brain has conjured up this story, using some of the information I learned in my art classes."

Mike took a sip of his drink. "That may be true but there seem to be details you wouldn't necessarily learn in an art class. Yes, you would learn about Homer's mother since she, too, was an artist and influenced Winslow. But would you necessarily learn about her dying in April of eighteen eighty-four? Have you checked to see if that's correct?"

"Mike. That's a very interesting question. It's possible that information might have been given in class but to be honest, I'm not sure." I snickered. "I do have to admit it's a rather obscure piece of information. I still think it's a product of my brain, working overtime."

Mike got out of his chair, walked over to the coffee table and picked up his iPad. He started poking at the keyboard. After a few moments, he used his finger to move the information on the screen. "Interesting. She DID die in April of eighteen eighty-four." He returned to his chair.

I finally came to the telling of the previous night's dream. When I mentioned the tall, dark, handsome fisherman and the evening at the restaurant, Mike sat straight up. "Well! Now, that's very interesting. Continue. Continue!"

"I don't know how to explain it but there's a huge connection between the 'me' person in the dream, whose name is Richie by the way, and the fisherman, Farin. The 'me' in the dream really knows nothing about him but there's that incredibly strong connection. It's crazy, I know. Have to tell you. I sure wouldn't mind having that kind of connection with someone that's not in a dream."

Mike shook his head and chuckled. "That makes two of us." He laughed. "Okay. You mentioned the Cape Elizabeth Lighthouse. Have you ever heard of the Cape Elizabeth Lighthouse?" A sneer came to his face. "Just thinking of validity again."

"I don't think so. But. It's possible when doing research for my first novel. Maybe I happened to see something on it or read about it. After all, that novel does take place up in New England."

"Well. Okay. Maybe so. But I still think there's a lot more to this than just coincidence." He paused for a moment. "All right, continue."

I looked at Mike with a sad expression and shrugged my shoulders. "Hate to tell you but that's where it ended last night. What can I say?"

Mike looked at me with an angry expression. "What!? No! No! What do you mean that's all there is? You have to be kidding. Okay! I tell you right now. I better be on your list of folks who want to know the WHOLE story. There's just got to be more to this. I can't imagine it ending where it has."

I looked at Mike and started to laugh. "Hey! How do you think I feel? I'm the one who's in it. You don't think I don't want to know where this is going? I have a feeling you are absolutely correct. And I'll keep you posted on future developments. It's like Joe at work said the other day. 'Enquiring minds want to know.'"

We both raised our Bloody Marys in the air and laughed.

*   *   *   *   *

That night I slept very soundly. There were no dreams. Mike knew I had to get up early to get on the road as it was about four hundred miles to just north of New York City. I'd be staying with Rick and Julian. Before I left, I gave them a call to let them know I was on my way.

I climbed on my bike and backed it out to the street. I got off and gave Mike a big hug before putting on my helmet and gloves. "Thank you so much for letting me stay. I really appreciate it."

Mike smiled. "Give me a call when you know you're on your way back this way. I could use another day off from work. And you know I want to hear more about how the dreams end. Like the great Paul Harvey used to say. 'And now you know… the rest of the story.'"

We both laughed.

As I headed down the street, I looked in my review mirror and could see Mike waving. Raising my left arm, I waved back. First stop, the nearest gas station. There was one just before I got on the expressway.

It was another sunny and uneventful day of riding. I arrived at Rick and Julian's around four-thirty in the afternoon. These guys I'd never met in person just chatted online for some time. I didn't want to impose, so I'd be leaving the next day.

They had fired up the grill and invited several of their friends over to meet me. Many of them had made online purchases of my two novels in print and asked me to sign them.

Of course, everyone was interested in my trip. They became extremely interested when I told them it coincided with some dreams I'd been having. I was impressed at how intently everyone listened as I told the story. Again, all wanted to hear about the ending on my return trip home. They all chuckled, regarding the possibility of another novel.

* * * * *

I really liked Rick and Julian and was pleased I'd met them in person. They extended an invitation to me to stay on my return trip.

Rick laughed. "You do realize if you don't stop and stay, our friends will kill us. They want to hear the ending to these dreams just as much as Julian and I do."

I thanked them for the stay. I also told them to tell all their friends how nice it was to meet them.

* * * * *

The trip to Boston was some two hundred and sixty miles. Actually, I'd be staying north of Boston with Eric and Sam. These were two more guys I'd met online yet never met in person.

Again, the story of the dreams had to be told. Eric chuckled when I'd finished. "Sounds like another book to me."

Sam got up and went to the bookshelf. He pulled two books down. With one in each hand, he waved them in the air. "You know you're not leaving without signing these."

We all laughed.

When I went to bed, I had another calm and restful sleep. There were no dreams, either.

* * * * *

Eric and Sam both expressed how pleased they were they got to meet me in person. They, too, were looking forward to my return trip and hearing the rest of the story. I told them how much I appreciated the invitation and thanked them again for letting me stay.

CHAPTER VI

I had called Bob before leaving to let him know I'd probably be there around noon. He said he was very anxious to see me. I'd met Bob some ten years prior about two years after moving to Atlanta after college. He was a super nice guy. I liked him a lot.

Bob left Atlanta about three years after I met him, being transferred to Portland with his job but we still stayed in touch. I was extremely fortunate he wanted me to stay with him the entire time I was in Maine. It saved a fortune in hotel bills.

I have a feeling Bob really liked me and wanted to get into a relationship. Yes, I liked Bob but the chemistry just wasn't there for me. I did know we'd be the best of friends for the rest of our lives.

Upon arriving, Bob had me park my bike in his garage. We unloaded the bike, bringing everything to the room he'd set up for me.

Bob pointed. "You can set your easel up over there. I think you'll have enough light from that window. If you need more room, we can move some of the furniture around."

I shook my head. "Bob. You've gone much too far out of your way. This is more than excellent. Thank you so very much."

We placed my large carryall and small satchel against the far wall. I'd hang my clothes in the closet later. Bob got several boxes to put all my art supplies in from the saddlebags. I put them under the easel. Now, all I needed were a few canvases.

Bob smiled. "Since it's still early in the day and if you're not too tired, why don't we go down to the art shop. You can get things you need. Then, we can go have lunch at one of my favorite seafood restaurants. How does that sound?"

"Bob. You're way too kind. I'd love to pick up a couple of canvases. And for your information, lunch is on me." I started to laugh.

"If you say so." Bob joined the laughter.

Going by the art shop, I bought several items I knew I could use like linseed oil and turpentine. I also bought four canvases of standard sizes. One was a twenty-four by thirty and the other three were twenty-four by thirty-six. I already had in mind what I was going to paint on the twenty-four by thirty. Standard sizes make it so much easier to frame them. Maybe four canvases was wishful thinking. But hey. I could hope.

It was around three-thirty when we arrived at Bob's favorite restaurant. There were very few customers. Getting a table out on the terrace, overlooking the ocean, was no problem. From the reaction of the waiters and staff, it was obvious Bob was a fairly regular customer.

The table where we were sitting had an umbrella to keep the sun off of us. The chairs were extremely comfortable and the view was spectacular. After sitting down, we made our drink orders when the waiter brought the menus.

Bob chuckled. "I'll tell you right now. Everything here is excellent."

When the waiter returned with our drinks, we made our order. The waiter was polite and slightly bowed as he left the table.

Bob turned with a smile. "So. How are things in Atlanta?"

I chuckled and for the next thirty to forty minutes while we were eating, we caught up on what had been happening in both our lives since last we'd seen each other. Bob kept bemoaning the fact he was going to end up single the rest of his life. I just reminded him of an old expression. 'You never know what's around the next corner.' That made us both laugh.

Bob took a sip of his drink. "So. What made you decide to come up here for a month-long vacation?"

I smiled and chuckled. "I thought I'd try my hand at painting the ocean." I laughed.

"What's wrong with that? Why is it funny?" Bob tilted his head.

I shook my head. "Bob. The ocean is one of the most difficult things to paint and make it look real."

"Well." Bob had a reassuring expression on his face. "You've come to the right place. The land of Winslow Homer. America's greatest seascape artist."

I'd been sipping my drink when Bob's comment made me almost choke and break out into almost uncontrollable laughter. I bent over and shook my head. "I'm sorry. I'm sorry. I couldn't help it."

"Okay. Let me in on the joke. What did I say that's so funny?"

I finally composed myself. "Winslow Homer. You said, Winslow Homer."

Bob's face scrunched up. "I don't get it. What's so funny about Winslow Homer?"

"It's the dreams I've been having."

Bob raised his right hand to get the waiter's attention. He was quickly at the table. "Larry. Get us some more drinks and when you see they're nearing empty, bring us more. My friend is about to tell me something I just know is going to be incredibly impossible. With what I'm about to hear, will require several cocktails. I'm sure."

We all started laughing.

I looked up at the waiter. "Larry. Bob is absolutely correct. Just keep them coming."

And so, the telling of the dreams began and ended with what took place in the restaurant. I looked right at Bob. "And that's the story so far."

"Wow!" Bob took a drink of his cocktail. "Wow! That's some story. Now, I understand why you laughed when I said, Winslow Homer. But what's interesting is there seemed to be a few obscure pieces of information in the story. That's odd you'd know those things. Like when Homer's mother died and the lighthouse. Have you ever been up here before?"

"Never. It's funny you should bring up those two things in particular. Someone else pointed them out as well. He actually checked and Homer's mother did die in April, eighteen eighty-four."

"Do you think the dreams are over?"

I stroked my beard with my right hand. "I don't think they are."

Bob chuckled. "Very interesting. Very interesting. You do know this sounds like another possible novel."

We both broke out laughing, raising our drinks up in the air and clinking them together.

Since we'd been having our cocktails at a leisurely pace, Bob said he felt fine to drive. We did have several cups of coffee before we left the restaurant. It was going on seven o'clock.

Getting home, Bob was going to fix dinner. I told him I wasn't hungry after eating such a wonderful late lunch. I also decided to turn in early. I was tired. Bob told me to sleep as late as I wanted. I had full run of the house. He'd be heading to work around nine. If I needed anything, he told me to call him on his cell phone. If for some reason I needed to leave the house, an extra set of keys and garage opener were on the hook by the refrigerator.

*   *   *   *   *

I got up early and started the coffee in the fireplace. I tried to be quiet as Uncle Winslow was still asleep or so I thought.

A voice came from the doorway. "I thought I smelled coffee." Uncle Winslow stood there with a big smile on his face.

I looked at him with a guilty expression. "I just thought. I just thought I'd get up early and fix coffee."

Uncle Winslow chuckled. "Have no fear. Your young man will be here shortly. I can guarantee it."

I was flustered. "But I. Well I. I just thought."

Uncle Winslow broke out into raucous laughter. I shook my head and joined in. Had it been so obvious?

Just then we heard the sound of a horse and wagon pulling up to the Studio. I looked right at Uncle Winslow. "Okay. Okay. You were right."

This made us both laugh even harder.

"Oh, my. Oh, my. This is too much for an old man. I've got to sit down." He continued to laugh as he went over and sat down at the small table. "For crying out loud. Go out there and meet your young man. I'll pour us all a cup of coffee."

I quickly wiped my hands on the cloth I had in my hand and with a smile ran out to meet Farin. I'd forgotten I still had on my art apron to prevent me from spilling anything on my clothes.

He climbed down from the wagon, took a few steps in my direction, stopped, looking at me with his hands on his hips. He looked me up and down with a huge smile on his face and began to chuckle. "Well. I can see someone would make a person a great wife." He flexed his eyebrows.

I immediately looked down and saw the apron.

We both broke out in loud laughter.

I smiled and looked into his wonderful eyes. "Farin. Welcome. So good to see you again." I walked toward him, extending my right hand.

With a big smile on his face, he walked to me and shook my hand. "Boo. It's good to see you again as well."

"Please. Please, come in. Uncle Winslow is pouring coffee as we speak."

"Just a minute. I brought a block of ice for Mr. Homer for his ice chest. Let me get it." Farin went to the back of the wagon and pulled out a large block of ice. "Picked it up on the way over here. Thought he might be able to use it."

He lifted the block and we both entered the house.

Uncle Winslow saw the ice. "Farin, my boy. Thank you. If you'll put it in the ice chest on the porch, I'd appreciate it."

They both went to the ice chest and Uncle Winslow removed a few things, so the ice would fit then placed them back in again. They headed back into the house.

Farin removed his cap. "Mr. Homer. Good to see you again, Sir."

Uncle Winslow turned toward Farin. "Welcome, my boy. Please. Please, come in and have a seat. You're just in time for coffee. Cream and sugar are on the table. When we're done, I'll put the cream back in the ice chest."

We all sat down at the table. Uncle Winslow was to my right and Farin was across from me.

I looked at Farin. "Would you like something to eat? I can fix us something."

Farin smiled. "Actually, I ate earlier this morning. I'm sorry."

I turned to Uncle Winslow. "How about you?"

Uncle Winslow just grinned. "No. I'm not really hungry. I'll eat something later on."

Uncle Winslow turned to Farin. "Farin. What's on your agenda for today?"

"I basically got everything I needed to get done today, early this morning. I didn't want anything to interfere with coming here and sharing time with you both. I still can't believe I'm really here.

The Studio of the great Winslow Homer. And I'm sitting here, having coffee with him. Wow."

Uncle Winslow chuckled. "My boy. My boy. You are way too kind. I'm glad you could visit. When we finish our coffee we'll show you around the place."

I kept staring down into my coffee cup. I was afraid to look up and see Farin's face directly across from me. I was so excited. My heart was beating so hard, I was afraid it would jump out of my body. What was it about this man, making me so crazy? It's totally illogical. I don't even know the man. And yet, I feel a connection with him I've never felt with another person. What is that? Am I insane?

Suddenly, I was drawn to attention by the sound of Farin's voice. "Boo. It really is so good to see you again. I've been looking forward to it for a very long time." He looked down at his coffee cup in slight embarrassment. "I know it sounds crazy and stupid but it's true. I believe even your Uncle understands. If he didn't, I doubt I'd be sitting here right now."

Uncle Winslow smiled, reached over and patted Farin's left hand with his right. "You're a very perceptive young man. I know there are many who would never understand which is sad."

Finally, finishing our coffee, Uncle Winslow led the way in, showing Farin the Studio. We first came to the area where we had the easels and canvases set up for painting. Of course, my easel was empty as I hadn't stretched a canvas yet, only arriving the day before. But Uncle Winslow had one large finished canvas set to the side and one on his easel he was still working on.

Farin looked at Uncle Winslow's paintings. "Oh. Mr. Homer. Your work is amazing. I feel like the waves could almost come crashing off the canvas onto the floor. You artists amaze me." He turned his head in all directions and then at me. "Okay. I know you're not here just taking up space."

We all giggled.

I put my hands on my hips. "Excuse me. I just got here yesterday. Geez."

Uncle Winslow broke in. "Actually, come over here into the sitting area." He led us into another room and pointed at the wall. There was the framed painting I gave to Uncle Winslow the last time I was there. I almost started to cry, seeing it hanging in such a prominent place.

Farin looked at the painting and then at me. "That's one of your paintings? And you did it over twelve years ago?" He looked back at the painting. "I am impressed. Mr. Homer has taught you well. Wow." After a few moments of staring at the painting, he turned to me. "I'm wasting your time. You should be painting. Get in there and paint."

We all just roared with laughter.

Uncle Winslow giggled. "We artists can't paint continuously. We do have to stop now and then. Now, come. Let's see the rest of the house."

When we reached the second level covered deck, Farin walked over to the railing and looked in all directions. "What a terrific view you have from up here. It's spectacular."

I pointed toward the shore. "If you like, we can walk down and you can see the ocean up close." I shook my head and started to laugh. "What a stupid thing to say to someone who's an ocean fisherman."

We all began to chuckle. It grew into loud laughter.

"Yes. Even though I'm an ocean fisherman, I wouldn't mind going down and looking at the ocean."

Uncle Winslow spoke up. "Why don't you young folks go down and look at the ocean and I'll get back to work on my painting?"

"Okay. We will. We'll be back shortly." I led the way as we went downstairs to the studio. As we headed out the door, I called back. "See you in a little while."

We reached the beach and walked out onto one of the rocks. We stood quietly for a while just taking in the view.

Farin snickered. "You know? I have to tell you. Everyone's perception of Mr. Homer is so wrong. They see him as a reclusive, self-absorbed hermit of a man, not caring about anything except his painting. If they only knew. I've been around him and you for just a very short time and I see and realize. He is a perceptive, considerate, thoughtful, caring, kind and loving man. I mean, look. He could've come with us down here but he didn't. He wanted you and me to have some alone time together. And whether or not you know it, he loves you very much. My uncles are like rocks. I sometimes wonder if they have any feelings at all. I'd hate to be their wives."

I snickered. "Uncle Winslow isn't really my uncle."

Farin looked hard at me. "He's not? You're kidding me."

"Nope. My mother knew his, back in the day and she thought it would be good for my career to study with her son. And because of the age difference, I should call him Uncle Winslow. Well, she was right about that. Rest her soul. I got a very good job in New York when they heard I apprenticed with him."

Farin was shocked. "He cares like he does for you and you're not even related. I'm amazed. I'm floored. Holy cow. What an incredibly, unselfish man he is."

"You're right. I enjoy his company and he has taught me so much about painting. I should've come back sooner. But you know how it is. You get all wrapped up in your work and time flies by. Before you know it, years have passed."

"Yeah. If you had come back sooner, I'd have met you sooner, you silly goose." He punched me in the right shoulder and started laughing.

I looked right at him. "That's true. But would we have been ready then? Were we mature enough then? Would we have appreciated what we truly have? Farin. I don't know about you but it's crazy. You and I know nothing about one another. But for me, there's this incredible and undeniable connection I feel for you. It makes no sense."

Farin giggled. "For me, it's the same and I can't explain it. I've looked forward to you coming back for so long. The feelings inside me grew and grew. It's one reason I gave you your name. I'd close my eyes and call your name in the darkness, pleading for you to come back to me. I know this is going to sound really crazy. But do you think it's possible we knew each other in a previous life?"

I bent my head down and started laughing. "No. I'm not laughing at you. I'm laughing because I've wondered the same thing."

"Boo. I feel so comfortable with you. Damn. Do you know? When I saw you in the restaurant last night, I wanted to run over and hug you so tightly, our bodies would have become one. Right now, it feels like my heart is joined to yours and they beat as one. I believe if something ever happened and your heart were to stop, mine would stop as well."

"Farin. I can't believe it. You and I have the same feelings, the same connection. I feel exactly the same way. What can I say?"

Farin turned and grabbed my shoulders and looked directly into my eyes. "Boo. Please, don't think I'm crazy. But. Boo. Boo. I love you, you silly goose. Boo. I love you."

I looked up into Farin's wonderful blue eyes and smiled. "Farin. I love you, too. I love you so much."

Farin pulled me to him and we hugged tightly. We held each other close, slowly rocking back and forth.

Farin whispered. "I thought I was going to die alone and unloved. And then. There you were. But then you disappeared for years and I thought I had lost you. My heart almost jumped out of my body when I saw you last night. I knew there was hope again."

My head rested on Farin's chest. "I know. I thought about you for years and when I saw you at the restaurant last night, I almost couldn't contain myself." I pulled back from Farin, looked up at him and smiled. "Okay. We're going to celebrate tonight. We're going back to the same restaurant and celebrate. That way, you nor Uncle Winslow nor I will have to cook." I started to laugh. "How does that sound? And since I have saved up for this visit, guess who'll be paying?"

We both laughed.

Farin smiled. "All right. Let me get back home, so you can get to work on your painting and I'll meet you and Mr. Homer tonight at the restaurant."

"Sounds great. How about around sixish?"

"Six it is."

We headed back to the Studio.

Farin turned to Uncle Winslow. "Mr. Homer. You really do have a terrific view here. This whole place is like a refuge from the world. It's so peaceful and relaxing."

Uncle Winslow smiled. "My boy. Those are just a few of the reasons I came to live here. I'll most likely be here till they drag me out after I drop dead."

We all just cracked up.

Suddenly, we heard a noise out front. Uncle Winslow went to check it out. "There's a wagon coming up. I wonder what he's needing or looking for?"

We all went out to see.

The man pulled up the wagon and called out. "Are you the incredible seascape artist, Mr. Winslow Homer?"

Uncle Winslow answered. "Well, I don't know about incredible seascape artist but I am Winslow Homer."

"Sir. I'm a photographer and I'd so very much like to take a few pictures of you here at your Studio. I was wondering if you'd oblige me?"

"Why certainly, young man."

"Thank you. Thank you, Sir. Thank you so very much." The man climbed down from the wagon and ran to the back of it, pulling out his camera equipment and started setting it up. "You have no idea how much I appreciate this." Within moments he was ready.

"If you will stand over here, so I can get a good shot of your face. Then the next one with you over there, so your Studio will be behind you."

"Would it be possible for my friends to be in one of the photographs?" Uncle Winslow gestured toward Farin and me.

"That would be excellent. Certainly. First. Let me get one of you alone."

Uncle Winslow stood with a smile on his face, his Studio in the background. The man smiled. "Perfect. Now. Hold still and don't move." He pulled out something from the camera, slowly counted then put it back again. "Excellent. Now. Everyone."

We all stood together. Uncle Winslow, me then Farin to my left. With the camera so close, it was obvious our faces would be quite clear in the picture.

"Now, when I say smile, I don't want you to move a hair until I say you can. So. If your nose itches or your eyebrow, please, scratch it now."

We all laughed then finally composed ourselves.

"Okay. Now. Smile." He pulled something from the camera and was silently counting. After several moments, he put it back. "Great. Now, you all can move over there." He pointed to a spot as he repositioned his camera. He took a moment to see the composition. "That looks terrific. Is everyone ready?"

We all in unison. "Yep. Let's go." We stood perfectly still.

He repeated the same procedure as we made no moves. When all was said and done, he called out. "Excellent. Excellent. I truly appreciate it. Thank you, gentlemen. Now, if I could get one more of Mr. Homer alone, that would be terrific."

In no time at all, he had taken a close portrait picture of Uncle Winslow. Finishing, he walked over and shook Uncle Winslow's hand. "It's an honor to meet you, Sir. An honor. I'll send you copies of the pictures in about a month or so."

"Would you like to come in for a cup of coffee?" Uncle Winslow smiled.

"Oh, no. But thank you. I really need to get moving. I have to get up to Portland to take some pictures up there. I do appreciate the invite, though. Thank you so very much for being so kind." He turned to Farin and me. "And thank you, gentlemen. Thank you very much."

We were all smiles as he packed everything back in the wagon, climbed on, waved and headed down the road.

I started to laugh.

Farin looked at me. "What's so funny.?"

"We just had our photographs taken and we have no idea who he is. No one got his name."

We all looked at each other for a moment in silence then totally roared with laughter.

CHAPTER VII

I woke up and peered over at the easel. I knew I was going to start a painting later in the morning. To the bathroom for a quick shower, shave the neck and brush the teeth. When I was done, I had no idea what time it was. I went to the kitchen. Bob was sitting at the table, eating some cereal. "Bob. Good morning."

"Well, good morning to you, too. I hope you slept well." He paused for a second then gave me a look. "Any dreams?"

All I could do was put a huge smile on my face.

"Well. I guess that's a 'yes'. I have to get in this morning but I want to hear all about it when I get back later on. Now, remember. If you need anything, you have my number. Call me. If you want to eat, eat anything you like. I'll pick up a few steaks to put on the grill for tonight."

"Sounds great. I'll be here. I'm going to start a painting."

"But you haven't even seen the ocean yet."

"I know. But I'm not going to paint the ocean right now. I have something else in mind."

"Really? Okay. I guess I'll just have to wait and see." He gave a big grin and flexed his eyebrows.

I wasn't hungry but I did fix a large glass of iced tea and went to the room. I pulled the twenty-four by thirty canvas out from the four canvases I'd bought and placed it on the easel. I stared at the blank white field for a while. Finally, a big smile filled my face.

I took my pencil and made a few sketch lines on the white surface. I stood back, looked, then walked back, putting more pencil strokes on the canvas. "Humm. I think that's perfect for placement." Over the next few minutes, I used the pencil to put a little more detail down. I smiled. It was now ready for paint.

I took one of the large jars Bob had given me and poured it half-full with turpentine. Next, I placed the brushes I expected to use in the jar. My paint rags I hung on the edges of the rack on the easel. In the other jar, I poured some linseed oil. I took the brushes out of the turpentine, cleaned them with the rags then placed them in the linseed oil to freshen them. The oil would keep the bristles pliable and from drying out.

I got out the new wax paper palette I bought and started applying colors from the tubes of paint. With my palette knife, I mixed a few colors. Dark colors first, building out to the lighter ones. The normal procedure with oils.

I started applying paint to the canvas. First, the dark background. I was actually surprised at how quickly the colors went into place. It was strange. Like I'd done this painting before and knew exactly how to paint it again.

Suddenly, I heard a voice in the house. It was Bob. "Are you still painting? I know you are. I can smell the turpentine." He began laughing out loud.

I had no idea time had passed so quickly. "Are you home early?" I applied a few more strokes of paint to the canvas, placed the brush in the turpentine to clean it, wiped my hands on the paint rag and headed out to see Bob.

"Hell no. Actually, I'm home later than I thought. I had to deal with a last-minute situation. It's resolved. Thank you, Jesus."

I shook my head. "Well, what time is it?"

"It's going on six o'clock."

"What!?" I was shocked. "I had no idea it was that late."

"You creative people. I swear. You get all wrapped up in what you're doing and have no clue what time it is. I wonder sometimes if you know what day it is or what month and year." He shook his head laughing.

"Bob. You're absolutely correct. We get all into what we're doing and have no clue of time or what's happening around us. That's how immersed we get into our stuff."

"I shouldn't complain or criticize. It's what makes you all great creative individuals. So. You obviously have started a painting. I don't dare ask what it is as I know you don't like anyone to see your work until it's finished."

I began to chuckle. "After dinner, I'll tell you about the dream last night and then I'm going to tell you about the painting."

"I have to admit. I'm chomping at the bit to hear more of this dream sequence. Seriously. From what I've heard so far, I sure as hell hope you write this as your next novel. I love the story." He reached into the bag he'd placed on the kitchen table and pulled out a wrapped package. Obviously, from the butcher shop. "Had these cut special. They'll go great on the grill. I also picked up a ready-made salad for both of us. Dressings are in the refrigerator." Bob headed out and lit the grill.

"Is there anything I can do while you're cooking the steaks?"

"Why don't you fix us both a drink. I sure could use one after today." He called to me from out on the deck.

After fixing our drinks, I headed out onto the deck and handed Bob his.

"Thanks. Okay. I know you like your steak medium-rare. They'll be done shortly. Run in and put the flatware on the table. They're in the top drawer to the right of the sink. Napkins are in the holder already on the table. Hope you don't mind paper." He snickered.

"Bob. I'm so sorry but I drank up almost all of your iced tea in the refrigerator." I called out from the kitchen as I placed the knives and forks on the table.

"No problem. I'd rather continue with cocktails. After dinner, I'll fix a bunch more tea to keep you happy tomorrow. It's easy. No sweat. If you'll reach up in the cabinet to the left of the stove, grab us two plates."

I placed two plates on the table and got several salad dressings out of the door of the refrigerator, setting them in the middle of the table. Just as I did, Bob came in from outside, carrying the two steaks on a platter, placing them on the table.

"I have to admit. Those do look terrific."

"Those two styrofoam containers on the end of the table are the salads. One for you and one for me. Feel free to dump it in your plate if you like."

As we sat and ate, Bob made comments about his work. "I swear. I had to deal with a governmental office today. MORONS! None of them know their jobs. None of them know what the hell they're supposed to do. IDIOTS! And we, the taxpayers, pay these imbeciles good money to sit on their asses and pretend to work. It irks me to no end. If it were up to me, I'd fire every last one of them and start out new. They're totally incompetent. There should be some law where we could sue those imbeciles for pain and mental anguish, having to deal with them."

I started to laugh. "Bob. Please. Tell us how you really feel." I couldn't stop laughing. "Hey. You're preaching to the choir here. I totally get it. Unfortunately, I'm afraid it's going to remain status quo."

Bob shook his head. "I know. You're correct."

After eating, we prepared another cocktail and headed into the living room.

"Bob. Thank you so much for dinner. There's nothing like a good steak. And you fixed mine perfectly. Thank you."

Bob sat down. "Okay. I'm ready. Let's hear it."

I sat and told Bob the entire dream from the previous night. After telling about the photographer, I stopped and got a questioning expression on my face.

Bob looked at me. "What?"

"I wonder."

"What!?"

I chuckled. "The photographer. He reminded me of Ansel Adams but that would've been impossible. Ansel wasn't born until around nineteen hundred."

"Nineteen-o-two." Bob started laughing. "Not exactly sure how I know that. I just do." He grabbed his iPad and punched at it. "Yep. That's correct. Nineteen-o-two."

It was strange. The whole time I told the story, I could feel the intense love between the two men. It was incredible.

After I finished telling all the updates to the dream, there were several moments of complete silence. Finally, Bob spoke softly. "Oh, my God. I know this may sound weird but I could feel the intense love they shared. I know it's only a dream but it's so real. Seriously. I hope your dreams continue. I'm extremely curious how this relationship is going to work out. Especially, with it being nineteen-o-one." He looked at me and grinned. "You don't have to tell me what you're painting. I already know."

I tipped my head with a questioning expression. "Really? Are you sure? Okay, Svengali! What am I painting?"

Bob wiggled in his chair with a very self-assured expression on his face. "You're painting..." He paused with a snicker. "You're painting Farin's portrait."

"Well, I'll be damned. You're absolutely correct. How did you know?"

Bob laughed. "For Christ's sake! Any idiot who has heard the whole story with the intensity and emotion in which you tell it would be able to guess. And here's another observation if you don't mind. I have a feeling you're falling in love with him, too. Yep. You're falling in love with a phantom in a dream. Now, ain't that dandy?"

"Oh, my God. Bob. You know what? I think you're right. I have a dream lover. What can I say?" I bent my head down, shaking it. "As ridiculous as it may sound, I really think you're right. Wow."

Bob broke into song. "'Dream lover, where are you? With a love, oh, so true.'" He began to laugh. "My apologies to Bobby Darin." He continued to laugh.

I shook my head and joined the laughter.

Bob smiled. "So. When do I get to see the portrait? When is it going to be finished? You know, I'm absolutely dying to see this person. And with your talent, I know the painting will be so lifelike you'd expect it to speak."

"Bob. It's amazing. The paint is just flying onto the canvas. Anyone would think I'd painted it before. At the rate it's going, I should be finished with it in just a few days."

"Well. I can't wait to see it."

Soon, it was time for hitting the hay. Bob indicated he didn't have to be in until noon. Before going into his room, he commented he was looking forward to the next episode of the dreams.

We both stood in the hallway, laughing.

*   *   *   *   *

Every time Farin had a chance, he'd come by the Studio. With Uncle Winslow being so understanding, it was like our refuge from the world. We could be ourselves without criticizing eyes, making judgments.

I'd started a seascape for Uncle Winslow to observe. What he didn't know, or at least I thought he didn't know, is I had started another painting. It was a portrait of Farin. The painting was going to take time because I wanted it to be perfect. I did plan to show it to Uncle Winslow after it was completed. Or what I thought was complete. Then, I'd like to have him critique it before showing it to Farin.

There were a few days Farin was going to be gone, helping out at the Cape Elizabeth Lighthouse. It was part of what he did and I had to accept that. The thing is, I knew I'd be returning to New York in a few weeks. Every time I thought about it, it made me crazy.

Finishing the seascape, Uncle Winslow was extremely pleased. "My boy, you have come a long way. I couldn't be more pleased with your work. There's nothing more I can teach you. You have your own style and it's excellent. You capture the shades and shadows, changes in coloring and your balance of subject matter is superb."

I was excited to hear his words. "Uncle Winslow. I owe you so much. The pittances my parents paid you and the small amount you have asked, letting me stay with you can never ever repay for what you have given me."

Uncle Winslow smiled and just spoke softly. "Remember, my boy. This has not been a street, going in only one direction. You'll never know the joy and friendship you have given me all the times you've been here. Your company has been gratefully appreciated. And there was a time when you were here to comfort me when my mother left this life. I'll never be able to explain in words how much that meant to me. Words will never suffice. So, let's not talk about who owes who." He paused for a moment. "And by the way, I know you're secretly working on another painting." He chuckled. "And I think I know what the subject matter is." A huge grin filled his face and he began to snicker.

I shook my head. "Uncle Winslow! I swear. Nothing gets by you. And you know what? I'm glad it doesn't. You're my mentor and confidant and no one will ever be able to replace you. If I can't discuss it with you, there's no one."

"You don't have to hide it in your room. Bring it out and paint it here in the studio. I promise. I won't look at it until you're ready for me to see it. Now, go get it and put it on your easel. And when Farin visits, we'll cover it with the cloth, so he can't see it until it's done. I'm sure that's what you intended." His huge smile continued and his eyes sparkled.

"You do realize, you amaze me. God was kind when He let the two of us come together." I went into my room and retrieved the canvas. Returning to the studio, I placed it on the easel. I looked over at Uncle Winslow, still painting his canvas. "Thank you. Thank you very much." I picked up my palette and brush and began to paint.

*   *   *   *   *

When I awoke it was morning. I had no idea what time it was but thought I'd get up anyway. After getting dressed, I opened the bedroom door and headed to the kitchen. From the smell of bacon cooking, I knew Bob was up.

"Well, good morning. I hope you slept well. How about some bacon and eggs?" Bob walked to the refrigerator, pulling out several eggs from the container in the door.

"Thank you. Only one egg for me. And yes, I slept very well." I walked over to the kitchen counter and poured myself a cup of coffee.

"The creamer you like is already on the table." Bob pointed.

"Okay. Do I need to ask?" He began to chuckle.

I sat down at the table and snickered. "You'll never guess who else is doing a portrait of Farin." I couldn't help but start to laugh.

Bob laid the spatula down on the counter and clapped his hands together. "Really? And how is his portrait turning out?"

"Believe it or not, I'm way ahead of him." I continued to laugh.

As we ate breakfast, I filled Bob in on the details of the previous night's dream.

Bob sipped his coffee. "I still say it's going to be very interesting to see how this relationship works in that time period."

"You do have a very good point. Things were very difficult back then. So, we shall see."

We collected the dishes and placed them in the sink. I told Bob I'd wash them later.

He gathered up everything he needed, his briefcase and headed out the door. "Check up in the freezer and pull out some pork chops. I'll pick us up another salad on the way home. Look for me around six."

There was a package of two very thick pork chops in the freezer. After taking them out, I found a very large bowl, placed them in it and filled it with cold water. I also did the dishes.

Now, it was time to continue working on the portrait. It took up the entire afternoon until Bob returned home. It continuously amazed me at how fast the paint went onto the canvas and all in the right places. At this rate, the portrait would be done in just a few days. I was sure of it.

It seemed no time had passed when I heard Bob arrive home. I called out from in front of the canvas. "Bob. Are you home early?"

"No. Not really. It's a little after five-thirty. Are you hungry? Did you eat anything today? No wonder you don't gain any weight. Damn!" He started to snicker. "Guess it's how the term 'starving artist' began. You never eat."

I stuck the brush in the jar of turpentine and headed to the kitchen. "I've been drinking iced tea all day. I'm so glad you made a big batch of it."

"Guess I'll make a batch every night, so you'll have it the next day. So, how's the portrait coming along if you don't mind me asking?"

"Bob. I swear to God. It's going faster and better than I could've ever imagined."

Bob giggled. "Well. I have an image of this guy in my head. I'm curious if what I imagine is anywhere near the reality."

"Give me a few more days. It should be done. Now, can I help you do anything?"

"Not a thing. Salad's in the styro boxes and I'll do a little work with the chops before I put them on the grill. I still can't believe you haven't eaten anything all day. Geez. I wish I had that ability."

We both laughed.

Dinner over, we sat down on the deck to just chill and relax.

Bob took a sip of his cocktail. "These dreams of yours have really got me thinking. They're incredible. I sure as hell hope you're writing all this stuff down."

"I have the computer out and tomorrow I'm going to diligently enter everything. I've already dictated much of the earlier stuff before I got here. For sure, I don't want to lose or forget anything that's happened so far. I'm also backing everything up on a thumb drive."

"By the way, I don't know whether I mentioned it or not but I have your two books. If you don't mind, I'd greatly appreciate it if you'd sign both of them." Bob gave a big grin. "Hey! You could be the next Hemingway, Steinbeck or Clancy. Who knows? Your signed copies will be worth a fortune." He began to giggle.

I looked at Bob and grinned. "As my mother would say. 'Don't hold your breath. You'd look like hell blue.'" I joined in the laughter.

CHAPTER VIII

The next morning, I got up and joined Bob for breakfast. I'd had a good night's sleep. Bob indicated after this day, he'd be off for several days. He told me to think of some things I might like to do on his days off.

All morning, I diligently entered all the additional information, regarding the dreams into my computer. I must admit. My dictation program saved me a huge amount of time. Typing is such a pain. When finished, I was very surprised to see how much information existed so far. I had no idea the story was going to be so extensive. What can I say?

By early afternoon, I got back to work on the painting. "Two more days. It should be done."

That night Bob wanted to take me out to eat. We returned to his favorite restaurant. I had no problem with that. The food there was excellent.

Finally, returning home, it was time for bed. Little did I realize it was going to be another night of dreaming.

* * * * *

Uncle Winslow had been so understanding. During the day,

we'd go out, sketching or stay in the studio painting. If it was possible for Farin to visit after his day's work, we'd go sit out on the rocks near the ocean and talk.

"Farin. In two weeks, I have to return to New York and go back to work. I hate the thought of leaving you. Do you mind terribly I'm so far away?"

Farin smiled. "You silly goose. I wouldn't care if you had to go back to the moon just as long as sooner or later you returned here to me."

"Maybe I could get a job in Portland. Possibly for the newspaper as an illustrator. I can also continue to paint and try to sell my works. Maybe Uncle Winslow would let me continue to rent my room from him. I'll ask him."

"What if you moved in with me?" Farin suggested.

I looked at him with an extremely concerned expression on my face. "Oh. No. No. No. That would NOT be a good idea. People would start to talk. You don't need that. It would be too dangerous for you. You're in a totally masculine profession. People expect artists like me to be weird and strange. Do you know what they would think if totally masculine started living together with weird and strange?"

Farin shook his head as he snickered. "Yes. Yes, I do. You make a very good point."

"Farin. You have your work and things you must do. It's your life. What we share must be secret and done when there's time and space to do it. I'll be happy whenever there's time available for us to share it. Just knowing you're out there and you care for me will keep me smiling."

Farin pulled me up to standing and he hugged me tightly. He whispered. "I can't believe I have been able to meet someone like you. God has been kind."

Farin indicated for the next couple of days he was going up to Cape Elizabeth to help out at the lighthouse. He'd let me know when he had returned.

For the days Farin was at the Cape Elizabeth Light, I worked diligently on his portrait. It was coming along very well.

It was finally the evening he was coming back and would come by for a visit. Again, we went down to the rocks just to sit and talk.

"You know, Farin. I believe one day, people will finally understand those like you and me are just as normal as everyone else. And I also know this may be wishful thinking but I believe there will come a time when those like you and me will be allowed to get married."

"Really? You have that much faith marriage could possibly happen?" Farin's face was filled with a surprised expression.

"Yes. Yes, I do. I think science will win out and all the religious propaganda will be tossed to the wayside." I looked at him and giggled. "But don't look for it to happen in our lifetime."

We both laughed.

I had a thought and had to work really hard to keep from laughing. "I have an idea. Let me know what you think."

Farin turned and looked straight at me. "What?"

"We could get married now."

He started to giggle. "And how do you propose we do that?"

"I can get a wig with long hair, put on a wedding dress and veil. That way we could get married." I looked at Farin with a huge grin on my face, trying hard not to laugh.

With his right hand, he began to stroke his beard. "Well." He paused for a moment. "I think the priest would look at you and your beard and mustache would give you away." He bent his head down and began laughing.

I started laughing with him.

I looked at Farin with a big smile. "You know I would marry you if I could. I love you that much."

He looked at me with a smile, leaned over and hugged me tightly. "Boo, you silly goose. If I could only explain, how much I love you as well."

We stood up, holding and hugging each other tightly.

With my right cheek against his chest, I spoke quietly. "Do you know how lucky we are? Some people go through their whole lives and never know love. You think you'll still love me when I'm eighty-six and your ninety?" I started to chuckle.

Farin just hugged me tighter. "I'll still love you when you're a hundred and eighty-six." He began to giggle.

*   *   *   *   *

I got up early and got the latest information on the computer. Then, I headed toward the kitchen. I could hear Bob, moving around and doing things there.

Bob saw me come into the kitchen. "I hope you're ready for at least two Bob McMuffins."

"Sounds great!" I went over and poured a cup of coffee. I also got the flatware out of the drawer and set the table.

Bob bit into his muffin, chewed and swallowed. "I have to hand it to McDonald's for inventing these things. I swear I could eat them all day long. Talk about fat and cholesterol, not to mention waistline. Geez."

"I know what you mean. It's one reason I don't dare go to McDonald's in the morning."

"Any more revelations last night?" Bob took another bite.

I bent my head down and chuckled. "Actually, they talked about getting married."

Bob almost choked and had to take a drink of coffee. "What!?"

"Yeah." I continued to snicker. "Jokingly, he said he was going to get a wig, wedding dress and veil."

Bob slapped his upper thigh with his right hand and broke out, roaring with laughter. "I can just imagine a bald guy with beard and mustache in a wig, dress and veil. The image in my head is absolutely hysterical."

"Farin thought it was funny, too." I paused for a moment. "It's amazing how future thinking they are. They have a realization that one day, same-sex marriage will come to pass and be legal."

Bob smiled. "You know. I have a feeling it will happen one of these days. I'll probably never see it in my lifetime, though." He shook his head. "So, how's the painting coming along?"

"I just might get it finished before I go to bed tonight."

"Oh. Wow. That means tomorrow I'll be able to see it. I love it." Bob got up and put his dish in the sink. "I have a couple of things I need to get done around here so why don't you go paint. Later on this afternoon, I'll run down and get some fried chicken. I know you love it. I'll get the sixteen-piece box."

I turned to Bob. "BITCH!"

We both roared with laughter.

While Bob did his chores around the house, I continued to paint. Strangely enough, I'd finished the canvas to my satisfaction just as Bob called out from the kitchen. "I'm headed in to get the fried chicken. You want me to pick anything up for you?"

I called out from the bedroom. "Wait a minute. I'll go with you."

"Well, aren't you going to try and finish the painting?"

"I'll finish working on it before I go to bed tonight." I placed the brush in the jar of turpentine, stood back and looked at the painting. I was very pleased but didn't want Bob to see it yet. I wanted to get away from it for a while before looking at it again. It's sort of like that old expression about being in the forest and can't see the trees. If I get away from my painting and come back at a later time, I can see errors, needing to be corrected more easily. My writing was exactly the same way. I closed the bedroom door and went to the kitchen to meet Bob. We headed off to town.

The chicken we bought was good but not as good as the chicken I could get in Atlanta. There's something about Publix fried chicken that's totally amazing. Nothing compares to it. I eat one piece and I can eat the whole box. I love Publix fried chicken. That's all there is to it.

Bob suggested if I actually did finish the painting, we might check out several places along the shore, possibly conducive to a painting. The idea was terrific.

Before going to bed, I stood in front of the painting for some fifteen minutes, looking at every detail. I shook my head and giggled. I, who hates to do portraits, had done an amazing job. I almost had to pinch myself to believe I'd actually painted it.

*   *   *   *   *

For the first time in my life, I was truly happy. I knew now, I wouldn't go through life alone.

Even Uncle Winslow recognized it. "My boy, I hope you don't mind me making a comment but I have to tell you. I'm so happy for you. Life's too short to worry about what other people think. Love and happiness are what everyone should be striving for in their lives. Not criticizing others because they don't understand."

"Uncle Winslow. You totally amazed me. But I should've realized you would know. Your keen eye doesn't miss a trick. I'm so glad you understand and you are happy for me."

He gave me a big smile. "I'm happy for the both of you. Just be careful, though. Critical eyes will never understand."

"I understand. Farin and I had discussed that. It was one reason I knew we couldn't live together. I was hoping you'd continue to allow me to rent my room from you. I'm thinking about trying to get a job in Portland. Farin told me even if I had to stay in New York, it would be okay. He would understand."

"I could tell Farin is a very understanding young man. You're both so lucky to have found one another. Whatever happens, I know you both will work it out." He paused for a moment. "Of course, you can stay in your room. That's not a problem. And I shall continue to enjoy your company. That will make me very happy. Now, one other question. How's that painting coming along?"

"It should be finished in a day or two. You'll be the first to see it when it's done. My stay here is almost over. When I get back to New York, I'll tie up loose ends then come back here. I'll immediately head to Portland and see about finding work. I realize with family money, I really don't have to work but I believe work is important."

"Well, my boy. It sounds like you have planned it all out. Excellent. I can't express how happy I am for you both."

Farin came by that evening to let me know for the next few days he was headed out fishing. One of his cousins was under the weather and he volunteered to take his place. He did tell me he'd be back before I had to leave for New York. He wanted to give me one last big hug before I had to get on the train.

Farin smiled at me and hugged me tightly. "I'll see you in a few days. Paint something nice." He turned and climbed up on his wagon. He gave me a smile. "Boo. You know I love you so much, you silly goose." A huge grin filled his face and his eyes sparkled.

"You know I love you, too." I called out, smiled and waved as I watched the wagon move quickly down the road. I shook my head and could hardly believe such an incredible man loved me.

Returning to the studio, I went over to my easel and continued to paint. The portrait would be finished by the next day. I could hardly wait for Farin to see it when he got back. All I could do is hope he liked it.

I got up early to work on the painting. I wanted to finish before Uncle Winslow got up. Just in time, the last dabs of paint went on the canvas as Uncle Winslow entered the studio.

"Well, aren't we up early? And what's the occasion?"

I looked at Uncle Winslow and smiled. "The portrait is finished."

Uncle Winslow stood there, hands on his hips with a huge smile on his face.

"Are you ready to see it?" My whole being couldn't wait to hear his comments.

"If you're ready to show it to me." He quietly spoke and smiled.

"Okay. Close your eyes."

Uncle Winslow closed his eyes and tipped his head back. "Let me know when I can look."

I picked the canvas up off the easel and turned it in his direction. "Now. Don't be nice. Be honest. Okay. You can look."

Uncle Winslow bent his head down and opened his eyes. His hands were still on his hips. He stood there silent.

I cringed. I said nothing but my stomach was doing cartwheels. I wished he'd say something.

Uncle Winslow's arms dropped to his side and a huge smile filled his face. "My boy, you amaze me. It's an outstanding portrait. Anyone looking at it will get a total sense of the man. And look at those amazing blue eyes. I really like the little hint of a smile you've given him. It reminds me of the kind of smile that's on the Mona Lisa. Now, mind you. The smile doesn't take away from his masculinity. I think it makes the painting more alive. It's a wonderful painting. Farin is going to love it."

"Oh, Uncle Winslow. You really think so? That means so much to me. If you truly like it, it has to be pretty good. That makes me very happy. I can't wait for Farin to see it. He'll be back in from fishing in a few days." My entire being was jumping up and down for joy. "Uncle Winslow. We're going to celebrate. Let's go in and have dinner at your restaurant."

"I'd like that. I'd like that very much. We can celebrate the completion of a fine portrait in oil."

I was so glad Uncle Winslow approved of the painting. I then knew Farin would like it. I grabbed my small-headed brush and dipped it in the black paint. On the back of the portrait at the top and below the wooden stretcher, I wrote. 'Farin, I will love you forever. Your Boo' I smiled and turned the canvas around, placing it back on the easel.

CHAPTER IX

Getting up the next morning, I looked at the canvas. I had to laugh. It was as if I'd reached into my dream and pulled out the painting. That's how close they were in likeness. I was really pleased. What really pleased me was knowing if Winslow Homer had seen my painting, he would have liked it and given it praise.

I headed out to the kitchen to see if Bob was up yet. He was making coffee.

"Okay. Are you ready for this?" I looked right at Bob.

"What's going on? The whole tone of your voice shows you're extremely happy. What is it?"

"The painting is done. It's not only done here but also in the dream. And are you ready for this? They look like carbon copies of one another. Are you ready to see it?"

Bob laughed. "Am I ready to see it? Do I need to come over there and slap you upside the head?"

I began to laugh. "I'll take that as a 'yes'." I turned and went to the bedroom to retrieve the canvas. Returning to the kitchen, I was holding the canvas in front of me with the back facing Bob. "Close your eyes. I'll tell you when you can open them."

Bob did just as I asked.

I turned the canvas around, holding it chest high. "You may look now."

Bob turned and stared at the canvas. He gave a loud gasp. "Oh… My… God. What an incredible painting. What an incredible man. Geez. He's a hundred times more handsome than I imagined. Holy shit! No wonder you're falling in love with someone in a dream. If I dreamt of someone like that, I'd fall in love, too, and never get out of bed. Wow! And I love that little… that little hint of a smile. It reminds me of the one on the Mona Lisa. Now, I'm not being critical. The smile seems to give life to the painting and it definitely doesn't take away from the guy's masculinity. Not a bit."

I let out a howling laugh.

Bob shook his head. "What's so funny?"

"You're not going to believe this!" I shook my head. "Those are virtually the same words Uncle Winslow said in my dream about Richie's painting. Yeah."

Bob began to laugh. "Really? Winslow Homer said the same things?" Bob formed a fist with his left hand, moved it up to his open mouth, breathed hard on it then rubbed his fist on his chest several times. "Brilliant minds do think alike, don't they?"

We both broke into loud laughter.

Bob continued. "That's terrific. It should also give you an idea as to how good your artwork is."

"I'm glad you like the painting. Let me go put it back in my room." I returned the painting to the easel then came back to the kitchen.

Bob was pouring coffee. "Would you like a cup?"

"Thank you. Thank you very much."

Bob poured coffee. "Seriously. I'm extremely impressed with the painting. It's so alive. And those blue eyes are incredible."

After breakfast, I grabbed my sketchbook and we headed out. Bob indicated he knew of several places that would most likely be of interest to me. We spent the entire day, driving to places along the coastline. At several stops, I did some quick rough sketches and took several pictures with my cell phone. I also made some notations on the drawings as to colors. Maybe the training Uncle Winslow gave in the dream had been passed on to me. I could only hope.

The ocean scenes were amazing. I could understand why anyone who wanted to paint seascapes would come to this area. It was obvious to me I'd be returning to several of these locations on my bike in the next few days. I'd bring my cell phone and take many pictures just as I was doing that day. I'd bring my camcorder and take some videos as well.

Arriving back home by late afternoon, Bob commented. "That should give you some ideas for a painting or two."

"You've got that right. This whole area is a seascape artist's paradise. I'll get started on one tomorrow."

"I'll start something for us to eat since we haven't had much all day. How do hamburgers on the grill sound?" Bob went to the freezer and pulled out a bag of premade hamburgers.

"Sounds great. What can I do to help?"

"Nothing. Don't you remember the old saying about too many cooks spoiling the broth?" He snickered. "You go and get your new canvas set up, so you can start painting tomorrow. I want to see a nice seascape in a few days."

Before getting in bed that night, I looked at the portrait again. I had to admit. It really was a good painting. Then, I began to ponder. I whispered. "Have I really fallen in love with a phantom from my dreams?" I smiled, shook my head and got into bed.

*   *   *   *   *

Farin had been gone for three days and I was finishing up a painting of the ocean. Getting up early, I went out and looked to the east. The sky was a mixture of reds and oranges.

I headed back in and fixed the coffee. Shortly, Uncle Winslow appeared. "I hope you made a big pot. I have no idea why but I didn't sleep well at all last night."

"Is there something wrong? Are you all right?" I was concerned.

"My boy, it's called getting old." He chuckled.

I laughed as well. "By the way, you missed an amazing sunrise this morning. The sky was ablaze with reds and oranges. Unbelievable."

Uncle Winslow shook his head in the negative. "Humm. Not good. There's an old saying. 'Red sky at night, sailor's delight. Red sky at morning, sailors take warning.' Usually, a sign of a storm coming up. Probably have one hit in a few hours."

I poured a cup for him and myself and we sat at the table.

"I looked at your painting this morning of the ocean. Looks like you're about finished. Just a few touches here and there. I like it. It's very good."

I smiled. "I couldn't have done it without you teaching me all you have." Hearing him tell me my work was good was a terrific boost to my painting insecurities. After finishing coffee and breakfast, I went in and began to work on the painting again.

Uncle Winslow was right. It was almost noon when a heavy wind and rain came in off the ocean. We had to quickly go and close everything up.

We both had just walked back into the studio to begin painting again when all of a sudden I got a terrible chill. I felt like I was freezing. I let out a shivering sound.

Uncle Winslow looked over. "What's wrong?"

"I just got this terrible chill all of a sudden. I'm freezing cold. I don't understand. I also feel a little sick to my stomach. Something's not right. Something's not right."

Uncle Winslow walked over. "Maybe you're catching a summer cold." He touched my forehead and then my arms. "My God. You ARE cold. You're correct. Something's not right. Let me get a blanket. Go lay in your bed and I'll be in in a minute."

I went in and laid on the bed. He covered me with the blanket. "I'm going to fix you some hot tea." He headed to the fireplace and hung the kettle over the fire.

Later, I went and sat in a chair in the studio, so I could watch Uncle Winslow paint. I drank hot tea all day and stayed wrapped in the blanket. Periodically, I'd peer out the windows to watch the storm. It lasted all afternoon.

"If you're not better tomorrow, I'm going in to get you something for it. You'll stay here and keep warm."

The next morning, I was still under the weather, so Uncle Winslow left and went into town. In the meantime, I finished the painting. I was very pleased and smiled. It was a decent seascape. I continued to drink more hot tea.

It was mid-afternoon when I heard the wagon pull up to the house. Shortly, Uncle Winslow walked through the door.

I looked at him. "I sure hope the medicine wasn't too expensive. I'm feeling a lot better. And I'll bet the roads are a mess after the storm."

Uncle Winslow looked at me with a concerned expression on his face. "My boy, come in and sit down. I need to talk with you."

I chuckled. "Oh. From the tone of your voice, this doesn't sound good. The medicine was a million dollars." I started to laugh. "Uncle Winslow. If I didn't give you enough money for the medicine, I have more in my room." I shook my head.

"My boy. It's not the medicine. Come in and sit down."

We walked into the studio and sat in the chairs across from one another. Uncle Winslow still had the same expression on his face.

I tilted my head to the side. "Okay. If it's not the medicine, what is it?"

Uncle Winslow bent his head down. "The storm. Yesterday afternoon. The storm was so bad, all the fishermen had to come back in. They got in late last night."

Surprise and joy filled my face. "Wow. That means Farin might be coming by this evening." I was ecstatic.

Uncle Winslow spoke in a scolding voice. "Let me finish!" He bent his head down again. There was a very long pause. "Several of the fishermen were down in town. Everyone knows. The storm was so bad." He paused for some time again. "While they were out, a huge wave hit one of the boats and one of the fishermen was washed overboard." Uncle Winslow lifted his head and he spoke quietly. Tears were streaming down his face. "It was Farin." His voice cracked. "Farin is..... dead." He was silent, looking at me.

I could not believe my ears. My joy had just been utterly destroyed. This could not be true. I let out a loud scream. "NO! NO! NO! NO! NO! He can't be dead! No! No! It's not fair! It's not fair! Farin! No!" I fell out of the chair and went rolling on the floor, pounding it with my fists. "No! No! It's not fair. Farin! Don't leave me! Don't leave me. I love you! Don't leave me! No! No! No!" I was screaming and crying.

Uncle Winslow knelt on the floor next to me, pulling me up into his arms. He was crying. "My boy. My boy. I am so sorry. They said they tried to save him but the waves washed him away and he was lost. I'm so sorry." Still sobbing, he pulled me close to him and hugged me tightly.

*   *   *   *   *

I woke up and let out a loud scream and started crying uncontrollably. "NO! NO! NO!"

Just then, Bob quickly opened the door and ran to the bed. "What's wrong!? What's wrong!?"

I let out a loud yell and continued sobbing. "He's dead! He's dead! He's dead! Farin is dead!" I screamed out again.

Bob sat on the bed and pulled me up, hugging me. "Oh, my God. What happened? Come out to the kitchen and tell me. I'm fixing you some hot tea."

We went out to the kitchen and sat at the table. Bob made the tea. As we sat and drank our tea, I began telling about the dream. It wasn't easy due to being so distraught. When I finished, we both sat silent for the longest time.

Through tears, I spoke. "Bob. I know it sounds ridiculous but I feel like I've lost part of my heart. I know it was just a dream but I'm completely devastated."

Bob just shook his head. "I have to tell you. Your dreams sound so real, you'd think they actually had happened. I was also struck by what happened that afternoon to Richie in the studio when he felt cold. With the connection, Richie and Farin had, maybe he was feeling the cold water as Farin was drowning in the sea. I swear. This whole thing gives me goosebumps. Damn." He looked over at me. "I'm sure the dreams are now over. I mean. Where could they go from there?"

"I know. Maybe they are. Maybe they are." I took a sip of tea. "Bob. I tell you. I feel like I've been hit by a truck. Yes, it sounds stupid but I feel completely washed out."

"Why don't you just chill the rest of the day. We can hang around here. There's a few more things I could get done while you catch this story up on your computer and work on your new painting."

And that's exactly what we did the whole day. Bob made ham sandwiches for lunch and some spaghetti for dinner. I was feeling much better by evening.

As I lay in bed that night, I couldn't get the whole story out of my head. I tossed and turned until finally, I went to sleep.

* * * * *

Uncle Winslow was so kind and caring for the next few days. He tried the best he could to get me to cheer up a little but the weight of losing Farin was beyond belief.

"My boy. Come work on another painting. It might help you get your mind off your thoughts. I know how you feel. I remember how it was when I lost my mother. I was so glad you were here for me."

With sad eyes, I looked at him. "Uncle Winslow, I'm so glad you're here with me. You understand like no one else ever could. It's like everything inside me is gone."

"I know. I know. Let me go fix you some hot tea."

For the next few days, I was like the walking dead. I didn't want to eat or do anything. My body felt totally empty.

As I lay in bed that night, I knew what I had to do. I lit a candle, got out some paper, pen and ink and began to write.

Dearest Uncle Winslow,

I knew of all people, you will be the one to understand. You knew the connection and love Farin and I had for one another. He was my life. He was my light. I cannot imagine going on without him. I see no light at the end of the tunnel.

Know I love you more than a real uncle and I have appreciated all you have done for me. Words will never suffice to explain how I feel. I love you. Please do not be angry. Just know I cannot find my way out of this deep abyss. So, I am pulling the dirt in over me. I love you.

Goodbye.

Your devoted student and loving nephew.

Richie

I folded the letter, blew out the candle and placed it on the mantel as I quietly left the house. I walked to the shore. I stood for a few moments on the rocks. I looked up into the night sky. "Farin. Wait for me. I'm coming. I love you." I slowly walked out into the cold ocean water and began swimming out to sea.

Finally, after a while, everything was calm and I saw a bright light ahead of me. I began to swim toward it. The water got warmer. I could see a shore. I became so excited. I saw Farin, standing on the shore with his right arm stretched out to me. I walked out of the water and before I got to him, I was somehow completely dry.

I slowly walked up to him and looked up into his smiling face and into his bright, shining, blue eyes. He grabbed me and hugged me tightly. I was so happy. Slowly, the light got brighter and brighter and brighter.

CHAPTER X

I woke up. Sadness filled my entire being. I quietly walked to the kitchen and sat down at the table. I put my head down on the table and began to cry.

Almost instantly, Bob was at the kitchen door and turned on the light. Without a word, he walked behind me, leaned down and hugged me.

I spoke quietly through my tears. "Bob. He wrote a letter to Uncle Winslow and walked out into the ocean." I slowly sat up straight and looked right at Bob. I smiled through my tears. "But I saw it. They're together. He swam toward a bright light. Farin was there, standing on the shore, waiting for him. They're together, hugging one another. Their love is still alive."

Bob wrapped his arms around me and gave me a hug. "Let me fix some tea."

"Bob. I'm so glad they're together. It's so sad. But at least they're together." I took a napkin from the holder in the middle of the table and wiped my eyes. "This may sound strange but knowing they're together again, makes me feel a little better." I gave a sad chuckle. "Also, knowing it was a dream makes it easier, too."

"You do realize how incredible this whole thing is. If you don't turn it into a damn book, I'll beat you to death." He tried to make me laugh.

I chuckled, wiping more tears from my eyes. "Okay. I promise. Just so you don't kill me."

We both laughed.

It was early morning but neither of us went back to bed. Bob called in sick. I just needed the day to recuperate and try to get back on my feet.

For the next two days, I worked on the ocean painting. I was beginning to feel like my old self again. Discussing it with Bob, he was glad I wanted to spend more time. He was thoroughly enjoying the company. I called work and asked them if I could extend my vacation another two weeks. They told me it wouldn't be a problem and to have a good time. They'd see me when I got back and to drive safely.

The seascape was finished. While Bob was at work, I took a ride down to the art shop on my bike. They had a fairly good selection of picture frames. Going through them, I found a twenty-four by thirty perfect for the portrait. I also found one for the twenty-four by thirty-six seascape. That one looked like gray weathered wood. They also had picture hanging wire and eye screws. The small stuff went into the saddlebags. The frames I strapped down to the bike with bungee cords and headed home. On the way, I stopped by a hardware store and picked up a box of one-inch brads.

Parking the bike in the garage, I looked through Bob's toolbox for a hammer. With frames, hammer and brads, I went into the house. Before placing each painting in its appropriate frame, I put the eye screws and picture wire on each one then used the brads to hold in the paintings.

I brought the paintings into Bob's living room and leaned them up against the fireplace hearth. There's a saying a frame can make or break a painting. Well, in this case, the frames made my paintings look amazing. I was looking forward to doing at least two more seascapes before heading back to Atlanta.

Shortly, I heard Bob coming in the kitchen door and called out. "Hey! Bob! I'm in the living room."

"Oh, really? What's happening in the living room?" He entered the room and looked over at the paintings. "Oh. Wow. They're fantastic."

"I wanted to mention. If you really like the seascape, it's ready for hanging."

"You're giving me the painting?" Bob spoke with surprise.

"It's the least I can do for letting me stay here and all the food you've been serving me."

"Wow! I know exactly where I'm going to hang it."

I chuckled. "The laundry room?"

We both roared with laughter.

"Remember. The paint's still wet and will be for almost a month. Also, I'm hoping to do at least two more before I leave. If you like one of those better than this one, we can switch them out. They're all going to be twenty-four by thirty-six canvases. Because of the subject matter, any one of them will look great in that frame."

"I gratefully appreciate it." Bob came over and gave me a big hug. "Let's hang it after dinner. I brought home two great Delmonicos to put on the grill."

*   *   *   *   *

For the next two days, I worked diligently on both canvases. I was determined. I was going to finish both of them before going back to Atlanta.

Bob came home that afternoon and suggested we go again to his favorite seafood restaurant. I was all for it. Bob wouldn't have to cook and I could pick up the tab.

As expected, the food was superb. All through dinner Bob commented how well things were going at his work. Dinner over, we continue with cocktails. Just as day was ending, we saw the moon, beginning to rise above the horizon.

"It's funny." Bob commented. "You've been here all this time, talked about your dreams, involving Winslow Homer and you haven't even gone down to Prouts Neck to see his Studio. It's now open to the public. Has been for almost two years now. And if you didn't know, you can call them and see how much the admission is. I've heard it's rather expensive."

"Bob. That's a great idea. The admission may be a little high but it's an historic site and they have to keep it going with upkeep and stuff. I'm sure the ocean-atmosphere isn't conducive to maintaining such a structure. In two days, you're only working half a day. I'll see about going down that morning on the bike. It shouldn't take too long to see the whole Studio. If it's anything like what it was in my dreams, maybe an hour. Two at the most. While you're at work tomorrow, I'll call the Portland Museum and see about making reservations to go. And on my way home after seeing the studio, I'll stop by and pick up the sixteen-piece box of fried chicken."

We looked right at one another and after a few moments of silence, we both broke up laughing.

*   *   *   *   *

The next day, I did call and spoke with a very nice lady named Margaret. I paid the fee, using my credit card. If it was at all possible, I wanted to meet at the studio, go on the tour then head out again. She indicated there were no tours scheduled and it wasn't often they gave a tour for only one person but it would be no problem. She said Fred would drive her down in his SUV. Fred also said he'd bring a small folding table, some folding chairs, his coffee pot and extension cord and we could have coffee while we talked before the tour. This, too, wasn't typical of a normal tour but with only the three of us, they could bend the rules a bit.

I thought what a wonderful idea and I'd bring some napkins and a bunch of sweet rolls. I'd also bring my favorite hazelnut creamer for the coffee.

*   *   *   *   *

The next morning, I took my time since we weren't going to meet until eleven o'clock. Arriving, I parked the bike and chuckled. "Well, I have the whole place to myself. My own private tour."

As I sat there staring at the Studio, suddenly all those emotions from the dreams began to come back to me. I could feel tears, running down my face. I looked again at the building and cried out. "I loved you so much." Shaking my head, I knew I had to get hold of myself. I took off my gloves and helmet and got off the bike. I paused for a moment to gather my wits, sticking my gloves in the helmet and then putting it over the top of the backrest of the buddy seat. I opened the saddlebags and pulled out the bags of sweet rolls, napkins and the creamer. I also grabbed my baseball cap and put it on my head.

Just then, an SUV pulled into the parking lot alongside my bike. An older man turned, looked out the driver's window and smiled. It had to be Fred. He opened the door and got out. "Well, hello, young man. How are you?"

I smiled and extended my right hand to shake Fred's. "Well. Thank you. You must be Fred. Let me help you get the table and chairs out of the car."

"Wonderful." Fred led me to the rear of the SUV.

The lady from the passenger's seat got out. "Hello. I'm Margaret."

I shook her hand. "Hello, Margaret. How are you? Oh. And if you wouldn't mind taking these, I'll help Fred with the table and chairs." I handed her the bags of goodies. "I want to thank the both of you for doing this for me. I realize it's totally unusual for you to do a tour for only one person."

She smiled, taking the bags. "Not a problem. Fred and I don't mind at all."

We set up everything near the front door. Fred soon had the coffee maker plugged in and we all sat down for a cup before heading inside.

"Where are you from and what brought you here?" Margaret smiled.

"I'm up from Atlanta. I came up for several weeks to paint the ocean." I giggled. "I'm on vacation."

She smiled. "So, you're an artist?"

Fred smiled. "Margaret here paints, too. She's pretty good."

"Oh, Fred." She bent her head down a bit in slight embarrassment.

I giggled. "Well, am I an artist? Maybe my good and close friends might say so. Others might not."

We all laughed as we continued to drink our coffee.

"Being an artist, I have a feeling you know something about Winslow Homer." Fred commented.

"Yes. I studied him in art history class at school and I've also done some reading on my own. He's amazing when it comes to painting the ocean. I thought since I was up here visiting, I might as well come see his Studio."

Fred looked over at my bike. "Really nice bike. You rode all the way up here from Atlanta?"

"Yep. Great ride. And seriously, the bike's extremely comfortable. Fred, you should go sit on it and see." I chuckled.

"If you don't mind, I'd love to. Always wanted a bike but never got one." He got up, went over and sat on the bike. "Wow. I see what you mean. This really is comfortable. I may have to rethink getting one." He gave a huge grin.

I'd noticed, during the whole time we were sitting and having coffee, Margaret seemed to take periodic stares at me with a questioning look on her face. Finally, she spoke. "Fred. Doesn't he look familiar?"

Getting off the bike, Fred was walking back to the table, looking at me closely. "Well, I'll be darn. Margaret, you're right. There's something familiar about him. Have you ever been here before?"

I was surprised. "Why, no. This is my first visit to the Portland area. Why do you ask?"

She shook her head. "You seem so familiar for some reason."

I chuckled. "Maybe I have one of those kinds of faces."

Again, we all chuckled.

She stood up. "I'll be glad to show you around if you're ready?"

I smiled at her. "That would be wonderful. My own private tour."

As I walked through the door, taking off my hat, I couldn't deny the feelings, rushing through my body. It was necessary to stop for a moment and get my composure before going any further.

Margaret saw the distressed look on my face. "Are you all right?"

I smiled and laughed nervously. "Yes. I'm okay. It's just something personal. I'm all right."

She came over and looked at me very closely. Slowly, her face changed from one of question to one of surprise and all-knowing. "Oh, my God. Fred! Fred! Look! Without his hat! Look!"

Fred came running from his chair. "Margaret, what?"

"This can't be." She uttered. "I remember now. We just got the restored photographs back about a month ago and I hung them along with the letters. They're in the sitting room with three paintings."

"Really? But what's so strange?" I questioned.

"You! I didn't realize it until you took off your hat. You're one of the people in the photographs." Her hand was over her mouth while she continued to stare into my face.

Fred looked at me closely. "Damn! Margaret! You're right! Holy cow!"

"What?" I shook my head. "What? That's impossible. Totally impossible."

"Come. Let me show you." She and Fred led me into the sitting room and pointed to the far wall.

I couldn't believe my eyes. There were the three paintings from my dreams with two framed and matted photographs, hanging to the right of them. To the left of the paintings were two more matted and framed items but I couldn't tell what they were from where I stood. The paintings were two seascapes and a portrait. A portrait of Farin.

My whole body went into shock. I started panting hard and I fell to my knees. I cried out. "Oh, my God! Oh, my God! No! No! No!" I fell completely on the floor crying out, pounding my fist on the floor. "They were real! They were real! Oh, God! They were real!" I completely lost myself and was crying uncontrollably.

"Sir! Sir! What's the matter? What's wrong? How can I help you?" Margaret turned to Fred. "Fred. Run get him his coffee."

Fred ran to the table outside and within moments returned with my cup of coffee.

I sat up, sitting on the floor and cried out through my sobbing. "The paintings! The pictures! I thought it was a dream but they were real. They lived! Oh, God! It's so sad!"

Fred handed me the cup. "I'll go and call for help."

I raised my right hand up. "No! No. I'll be all right. I just need to calm down and collect myself. You have no idea what a shock this is to me."

Fred reached down. "Let me help you up and let's go sit down."

"Please. First. Let me go see the paintings and the photographs. Everything here."

"Why certainly."

I stood and we walked slowly over to the wall. Soon, we were standing in front of the collection.

Margaret looked at the old photographs, mounted in black frames with gray matting and then back at me. "It is. It's you in the pictures. But how can that be? How can that be?"

Fred took a quick look. "She's right." He took a quick look at me then back at the photographs. "Yep. She's absolutely correct.

That guy in the middle is definitely you."

She looked closely again at the photographs and then back at me. "I don't understand. But from your reaction to all this, you seem to have some explanation. You must know something about this."

I got close to the photographs and with the finger on my right hand, I touched the glass, covering the picture where Farin's face was in the photograph. I began sobbing. "I loved you so much. Farin, I loved you so much."

Margaret wrapped her arms around me. "It'll be all right." We moved back from the photographs.

Through tears, I spoke as I looked back at them. "If you only knew. But you're not going to believe me. It's so fantastic and impossible. Right now, I'm so shocked and astounded, I can hardly believe it myself." I pointed to the tall man in the photographs. "That is Farin. His is the face in the portrait. This short guy in the middle is me and the man on the other side of me is Uncle Winslow." I paused for a moment. "It's funny. In the dreams, I never saw the 'me' person. I heard descriptions from others in the dreams but I never knew what I looked like in the dreams."

"This seascape I did and gave to Uncle Winslow before I went to work in New York." I pointed to the one on the right of the portrait. Then, I pointed to the one left of the portrait. "This is the one I had just finished the day I found out about Farin." I turned to the portrait. "I did the portrait for Farin but..." I paused in the remembering of the dream. "But I thought they were just dreams. I didn't know it was real."

I looked at the portrait. "If you look on the back, I had written with black paint at the top of the back of the canvas. If it's still there. 'Farin, I will love you forever. Your Boo'"

Fred walked up and carefully removed the painting from the wall and turned it around. There on the back of the canvas were the words I'd just spoken.

Fred and Margaret looked at one another and then at me. Fred spoke. "Young man, we all need to sit down and talk. Something's going on here that's beyond belief. And there's part of this we know you do not. Like the letter that was with all these items by Winslow Homer. And a goodbye letter to Homer from his student. They're right there." He pointed to the two matted and framed items to the left of the paintings.

I was shocked. "My letter to Uncle Winslow? The one I wrote to him before I..." I bent my head down in surprise. "Oh, my God. Oh, my God." I was still crying.

Fred rehung the painting. "I think we all need to go have a seat. I'll fix some more coffee and we can have a long talk. To be honest, I think I'd like something a lot more potent than coffee but I guess the coffee will have to do for now."

We went out front and sat down. Fred went and started another pot of coffee.

I suggested. "Before we start into this. I need to call my friend where I'm staying and ask him if he'll bring a painting here. One I completed just recently. The paint on it isn't even dry yet. I think once you see the painting, you'll totally understand."

"Certainly." Margaret added. "This is incredible. I'm overwhelmed and we haven't even heard the story yet."

CHAPTER XI

I got out my cell phone. "Bob. You're home from work. Great. Listen. Could you do me a huge, enormous favor? The portrait. Could you bring it down here to the Homer Studio? Yes. I know you'll be careful with it. If you can lay it down, so nothing can fall on it or lean against it, it will be fine. Okay? Cool. Yes. You are NOT going to believe what has happened. You'll be totally on the clue bus when you get here. See you shortly. And don't rush and get in an accident. Yes. My bike is out front."

As we sat there, I began to tell the story of the dreams, trying not to leave out any details. Fred and Margaret sat there, listening intently. When it was finished, Margaret was crying and Fred's head was bent down in contemplation.

Finally, Margret spoke quietly. "Oh. That's so sad. So sad. I hurt inside, it was so sad. So much now is becoming so clear. And he called you, Boo." She smiled. "He must have loved you very much. And Richie, it was so obvious you loved him as well to do what you did. No wonder you were so distraught when you saw the collection."

"Yes." I shook my head. "That's right. I did sign the letter I wrote to Uncle Winslow."

"Yes. Let me show you." She quickly got up, went in and removed one of the photographs from the wall and brought it to where we were all sitting. She turned the framed picture around, so I could see the back. A place had been cut out of the backing for the picture, so what was written on the back of the photograph could be seen. There, in black ink, were the words. 'Me, Richie, Farin'. Since Uncle Winslow had written it, it was totally obvious I had been Richie.

Margaret spoke again. "There was so much we never understood about the paintings and photographs and of course, the letters. We knew nothing of the circumstances of anything. All we could do is conjecture. But now, after hearing all this, much of the puzzle is coming together."

Just then, we saw Bob's SUV pull up and park.

"That's Bob. I'll go meet him."

"I'll fix him a cup of coffee." Fred called out.

Bob got out of his SUV and went to the back. I joined him. Before he unlocked it, he looked at me. "What has happened. Your eyes are so red. Have you been crying? What has happened?"

"Bob, I swear you're NOT going to believe what has happened. Here. Let me carry the painting."

We got the painting and headed over to the table where Margaret and Fred were sitting. They stood up and introductions were made. I was finally standing in front of Margaret and Fred and turned the painting around, so they could see it.

Both let out a gasp.

Margaret put her hand up to her mouth. "Oh, my God!" Margaret kept staring at the painting. "It's the same portrait! Exactly like the one here!"

Bob looked strangely at me. "Just like the one here?"

Margaret grabbed Bob's arm and led him into the Studio right to the collection.

He looked across the room at the wall. "HOLY SHIT! Oh. Excuse me. Pardon my French. You have to be kidding me! NO WAY! Really? Oh, my God! They were real. Your dreams were real! Holy Shit! I think I need a drink."

He and Margaret came back to join us.

Fred snickered. "Bob. I heard your comment. All I have is coffee right now but I sure as hell know exactly what you mean. I said the same thing."

We all laughed.

Bob shook his head. "Do you know how amazing and incredible this is? Wow."

I looked at Fred. "I know the Studio has stayed in the family for all these years but how is it the letters, photographs and pictures that I… Richie… painted survived?"

Fred smiled. "That could be a grace. The paintings were hanging, basically where they are right now. They did have to be cleaned and rehung after the renovation. That was after the Portland Museum acquired the property. Now, the photographs were stuck in the back of the portrait, between the canvas and the wooden stretchers with the faces of the photographs turned in, so no one could see what they were. The two letters were stuck behind one of the two seascapes the same way."

Bob questioned. "Two letters?"

"Yes. They're to the left of the paintings. Let's go see them." Fred led the way.

"I didn't read the letter Uncle Winslow wrote yet." I shook my head.

Bob walked over and started reading the letter on the bottom. "Oh, Geez. That's the one you wrote to Uncle Winslow before taking your final swim." He looked around at the faces displeased at his comment. "Sorry. I realize it is a truly sad story, but I was trying to bring a little levity to this whole thing. Sorry."

I chuckled. "Bob, we forgive you. We knew you meant well." I looked at the letter on the top. "This one was written by Uncle Winslow." I read it out loud.

"'To all concerned, from now and forever.

The three paintings here, the two photographs behind the portrait, the letter from my student that is behind one of his paintings and the one you are reading right now I want all of them to remain together. They mean more to me than my own works. Today, in this time, none of you will understand their significance and that doesn't matter. They are part of my legacy. An important part. A part none of you know of or would understand.

Last night I had a dream and saw them standing together, smiling at me. It made me happy.

Maybe one day, down the road, someone will put this puzzle together and the story will be known. Maybe it will happen, during a time of understanding, a lack of ignorance, a lack of intolerance and a lack of bigotry. I can only hope.

Winslow Homer'"

Everyone was silent for a few moments.

Bob quietly spoke. "He had a dream they were together. Amazing." He looked at me. "Just like the one you had. Damn. It's possible maybe that day of understanding has finally arrived." He was silent for just a short while and then he started again. "You know what? This is so amazing, I'm going to contact my friend Ralph at the TV station. He just might want to come out here and do some interviews and report this story. I mean, you all have to agree. It's totally fantastic."

Margaret was all smiles. "Wow. That would be a wonderful idea. And think of the free publicity for the museum and the Studio."

Fred chimed in. "You do know, if he does report the story, there are going to be a bunch of 'naysayers'."

Margaret looked at Fred, speaking authoritatively. "Who the hell cares! There are ALWAYS those kind of people. I swear some of them wouldn't believe it if Jesus showed up on their front lawn. I don't care about those ignorant and intolerant folks. There are too many who won't scoff at this. THOSE are the ones of import."

Bob snickered. "Wow! Margaret! You go, girl! You're so right. There are always going to be those who would never believe. And of course, with this kind of story, there's going to be an outpouring of those bigoted and intolerant religious fundamentalists. It's sad. Those morons."

Fred chuckled. "Hey, Bob. Yeah. Tell us how you really feel about those fundamentalists."

We all roared with laughter.

Bob shook his head. "I'm still trying to wrap my head around this and get a grasp of the whole thing. Let me call Ralph."

While Bob made his call, Margaret stared at the portrait I had done. "To me, this is so incredible. And it's so sad. Two people had found love only to die soon afterward. So sad." She turned to me. "Do you think it might be possible to hang your portrait next to the other one as a loan for a while? It enhances the story so much."

I was totally floored by her comment. "My painting? Hanging here? In Winslow Homer's Studio? Really? Wow! That would be such an honor. What can I say? I'll donate it to the Studio if you like?"

Bob returned with a huge grin on his face. "Ralph is going crazy about coming and talking. I told him to call you and set it up when it would be convenient for you all. I know you have your schedules."

Margaret turned to Fred. "What if he comes like two hours before we open. That would get him here at nine."

Fred flexed his shoulders. "Sounds great to me. Bob, can you call him back and see if tomorrow morning would be satisfactory? If that's too short a notice, we can work out a day next week."

Bob smiled. "Give me a sec." He went outside. Shortly, he returned and had an even bigger smile on his face. "Nine it is. Tomorrow morning. Everyone be here with bells on. He mentioned for us to watch the six o'clock news tonight."

I let out a yell. "YeeeHaw!!"

We all laughed out loud.

Margaret turned to Fred. "Don't we have a nail and hammer somewhere around here. I want to hang this new portrait up next to the other one. We can shift the seascape and photographs over."

Fred got up. "Actually, I've got my toolbox in the car." He went out and in no time at all was back. "How's this?" He held up a nail in one hand and a hammer in the other as well as a measuring tape.

When all were in place, we all stood back and looked at the collection.

"Wow." Fred shook his head.

Margaret smiled. "What an amazing collection."

Fred shook his head. "What an amazing story. Yeah."

Shortly, we all gathered up our things and headed out. Margaret and Fred to the museum and Bob and me to his house. Fred put the table and chairs in the Studio, knowing we'd be using them the next day. We were all looking forward to it.

Before the six o'clock local news ended, Bob's friend came on the screen. "Ladies and gentlemen." He smiled. "Ralph Aker here. I'm going to tell you. Tomorrow evening I may have a report that's going to knock your socks off. It's one totally impossible to believe. It took place over a hundred years ago, right down in Prouts Neck, Maine, at the Studio of the great American artist, Winslow Homer."

"If it pans out, there will be many who will scoff at the story. That will be your choice. But others will see and hear something truly fantastic. It has to do with Mr. Winslow Homer, a young student visiting him in nineteen-o-one and a local fisherman named Farin. And from what I can tell so far, regarding this story, I have a feeling I'll be doing a one-hour special with interviews and commentary."

"Tomorrow at nine in the morning, I'll be at the Studio, finding out about something people write books about. It should be very interesting. So, check out the news tomorrow evening for my report. This is Ralph Aker. Good evening."

I looked over at Bob. "Bob. What if this is a flop? I'm nervous right now and it hasn't even started yet."

"Hey! Just be you. Tell the story like you've told all of us. Now, there may not be enough time for your whole story. That might have to wait for Ralph's special. But he's a great reporter. He'll ask the right questions. Don't worry. He's a total professional at his work."

That night I went to bed extremely apprehensive. I laid there, tossing and turning, wondering how the next day was going to turn out. I've no idea what time it was but finally, I went to sleep.

*   *   *   *   *

Everything was bright. Slowly, it began to diminish. That's when I saw them in the distance. It was Farin and Richie, standing next to one another, big smiles on their faces and looking in my direction. And not too far behind them, was Uncle Winslow with a big smile on his face.

Richie took two steps forward. "It's time. It's time and you're going to tell our story. Where you are, people are much more understanding than when we were alive. There will be those who will embrace our story." He chuckled. "And yes. There are still those who won't. But thank goodness. Those who won't are slowly diminishing. Tell our story and let them know. We are together and happy."

Richie returned, standing next to Farin. They both gave me a huge smile. After a moment, they all turned around and slowly walked into the bright light. Soon, all three were gone.

CHAPTER XII

I sat straight up in the bed. Early dawn's light was coming through the window. I spoke in a whisper. "Wow. No greater love. Wow. And they're happy. And Uncle Winslow is there with them." A big smile filled my face even though tears were streaming down it as well.

I turned and looked around the room. I wondered if I'd possibly be able to go back to sleep again. I started thinking about what was going to happen at nine o'clock and I knew. There was no way I was going to be able to go back to sleep.

I got up and headed to the kitchen. That's when I saw Bob sitting at the table. "What are you doing up?"

"I'm thinking about later on this morning. I couldn't sleep."

I started to laugh. "I see you fixed the coffee." I went over and poured myself a cup. "Okay. Are you ready for this? Had another dream and I know it's the last one."

A shocked look filled Bob's face. "What? Another one? Really? Your kidding?"

"Nope. I saw both of them in a bright light. They're happy and glad their story is going to be told. Uncle Winslow was there, too.

I could see all of them clearly as they smiled, turned and finally disappeared into the bright light."

Bob spoke softly. "Wow. I think that's phenomenal. And you know what? They deserve to have their story told. Maybe it will help people understand love is diverse and stretches in many directions." He paused and shook his head. "And it even goes beyond death."

I looked directly at Bob. "Bob. That was a wonderful thing to say. I think that's exactly what they wanted to express and have people understand."

"I know this is going to sound really stupid but why don't we get ready and go down to the Studio. I see no need to hang around here. We could hang around just as easily down there."

"You know? I feel exactly the same way. Let's do it."

On the way, we stopped and got a huge box of donuts and sweet rolls to make sure we had enough for everyone.

It was around seven-thirty when Bob and I arrived at the Studio. We pulled into the parking lot. We were the only ones there.

"I guess we really are early." Bob began to snicker.

I couldn't help it. I started laughing as well.

Just then, we saw Margaret and Fred, arriving in Fred's SUV. They got out and headed our way.

Fred came walking over to the car, shaking his head. "I think you two are just as wound up as Margaret and I are. Come on. We'll set everything up like we did yesterday and I'll make a big pot of coffee. I have extra chairs in the car."

Bob and I left the SUV, bringing the donuts and rolls.

Soon, the table and chairs were all set up. We sat down to have a cup.

We'd been sitting for only a few minutes when we saw another car slow down and started to slowly pull up into the parking lot next to Fred's SUV. Fred spoke out. "I wonder who that could possibly be."

Bob commented. "I know it's not Ralph. He'd be in the TV station's van and most likely park on the street."

Fred got up. "I'll go see who this might be."

We watched Fred walk over to the driver's side of the car. The car door opened. That's when we heard Fred gasp and cry out.

"Oh!… My!… God! Folks! I swear! You are NOT going to believe this! Young man, please, come. Join us for some coffee."

We watched the man get out of the car. He turned and headed to the table. When everyone saw his face, we all quickly stood up in shock and there was mass hysteria.

I was totally blown away.

The man walked up, smiled and looked at me with intense blue eyes. He spoke quietly. "Boo, it's you. My, God. Boo. It's really you."

Bob had been standing but immediately sat down in his chair. "I swear to God. I really think I'm going to need a drink."

Bob's comment brought everyone back to reality. Everyone laughed. Even the handsome stranger.

Margaret fell back in her chair and began to get crazy. Tears started running down her face. "I don't believe it! I don't believe it! I don't believe it! Someone pinch me! Is this really happening? I don't believe it! The dead have come back to life!"

Fred seemed to be the only one who had it together. "May I get you a cup of coffee and a sweet roll? Mr...."

The handsome man, with dark chocolate-colored hair, beard and mustache, smiled. "I'd love a cup. And the name is Brandon. Brandon Summers."

I stood there with my mouth wide open unable to utter a single word.

Brandon looked at me and chuckled. "Boo. Don't you recognize me? I know you do. And I also know you and I have a lot to talk about."

I finally gathered my wits about me. "You called me Boo. Don't tell me you were having dreams like I was? Holy cow! This is beyond impossible." I looked at Bob. "You do realize your friend Ralph is going to flip out."

Bob took a sip of his coffee. "Hey! I'm flipping out! You're right. This IS beyond impossible."

Margaret jumped up. "Mr. Summers. Before you drink your coffee, you must come see." She led Brandon into the Studio and pointed at the wall. We all had followed.

Brandon stared at the paintings then slowly walked toward the wall. He looked at the two photographs. "I remember when the photographer took these pictures. At least the 'me' in the dream did. And Boo, there you are. And there's your Uncle Winslow." He paused for a moment. "Oh, my God. It's me. I look like me. I mean me now. This is crazy. I never knew what I looked like then.

I could see everyone else but I couldn't see me. I never knew what I looked like in the dreams."

I shook my head and began to snicker. "That's exactly what I said when I saw myself in the photographs."

Brandon then moved left to the two portraits. He smiled. "These are very good. Extremely flattering." He got very close to the one on the left. "This one looks quite old."

"Yes. Richie did it for you but you never got to see it." I commented.

He got very close to the one on the right. "This one seems to not be quite dry. Boo. Did you just do this one recently?" He turned and looked at me.

"Yes. I finished it not too long ago. I loved you so much I couldn't help but paint it." The words coming from my mouth shocked me. I looked directly at Brandon.

Brandon was looking directly into my eyes. A huge smile filled his face. "I know. I know you did. As much as I loved you."

Margaret began to cry. "But it's so, so sad what happened to both of you. You had your whole lives ahead of you. And it didn't get to happen. That is so sad." She continued to sob.

Fred wrapped his arm around her. "It's all right, Margaret. It's all right."

Brandon moved more to the left past the ocean painting. He read the framed letter that was written by Homer. He then read the letter beneath it. "Boo. For you to do what you did, shows you loved me more than anything. You made the supreme sacrifice for love. I had a dream last night. I believe it was the final one. They were both smiling at me. Do you know? Even your Uncle Winslow was standing a little ways behind them. They told me I needed to tell their story. Then, slowly, they all walked into the light." He paused for a moment, looking back and forth at the entire collection. "I hope you all realize. There's an amazing story in this collection."

The silence was incredible. No one spoke a syllable.

Bob finally spoke. "Brandon. How is it you showed up here this morning?"

Brandon turned around. "I happened to be watching the six o'clock news last night. And what I heard, in the last short report, totally bowled me over. I thought I was going crazy because of the dreams. But when the reporter spoke the name, Farin, along with a connection with the Winslow Homer Studio and a story that took place over a hundred years ago, I knew there had to be some connection. His comment he'd be here at nine in the morning made me realize I needed to be here, too, so I could put the puzzle together. So, here I am. Early. I wanted a good seat."

We all broke into raucous laughter at his comment.

Fred spoke. "Brandon. I think your seat is definitely going to be in the front row. Okay, folks. I've got to have more coffee and mull this over."

We all headed back out front and sat down.

Bob took a sip of his coffee. "Brandon. What do you do? What kind of work?"

"I'm a financier and stockbroker. Used to live in New York but it got too crazy there. With today's technology, you can do this kind of work almost anywhere. I opened up a small office in Portland. For some reason, I felt a kinship with this area."

"Interesting." Bob took another sip. "I'd like to get your phone number before you leave today. Been looking for someone to help me invest some money."

"I might have to have you invest some of my money, too." I smiled.

Fred chuckled. "If his investing talents are as good as his looks, he should be pretty well off."

Everyone chuckled.

It wasn't long until Ralph showed up with his crew. Bob went to meet him. Shortly, they walked up, Ralph with his microphone equipment and his cameraman with the shoulder cam. Introductions were made all around.

Ralph looked around at everybody. "Now, Bob did fill me in on some of what's going on here. But maybe one of you could hit the high points. Someone who knows most of the story."

Everyone looked at me.

"Not a problem." I paused for a moment. "To let you know, this whole thing began for me as a sequence of dreams. I also now realize, Brandon was having the same dreams but from his point of view. It started out with an eighteen-year-old artist from Boston, coming to study with Winslow Homer back in eighteen eighty-three."

For the next thirty minutes, I told a slightly abbreviated version of the dreams. Then I commented. "I had no realization the dreams were connected to reality until I walked in here yesterday morning and saw the paintings and photographs."

"I'd like very much to see the paintings and photographs." Ralph spoke calmly.

Margaret led the way. "Right this way."

We all followed.

Ralph and his cameraman stood back, looking at the collection. Then, they walked closer to the wall. Ralph looked at the two portraits. He examined the one on the right. "This one looks like it isn't even dry yet."

I responded. "You are correct. That one I finished just recently."

He then looked at the portrait on the left. "This one looks quite old."

Margaret spoke. "Yes. It belonged to Winslow Homer."

Ralph stood back and compared the two portraits. He raised his right hand up to his chin. "You do realize. This is amazing. I'd swear both of these portraits were done by the same person. The style and technique are exactly the same." He turned and looked at me. "And you say you completed this one just recently? Interesting. Very interesting." He stared hard at Brandon. "And both paintings are of you. Interesting. Very interesting."

He went and looked at the two photographs. "Okay. Where did these two photographs come from?"

Again, Margaret spoke up. "They were found in back of the original portrait. They are over a hundred years old. We had them restored recently. The man on the left in both photographs is

Winslow Homer."

Ralph continued to look at the photographs. "But the other two men." He paused and turned, staring very hard at Brandon and me. "The other two men are these two men."

"Okay, people. This has to be the most elaborate hoax I've ever heard of or it has to be one of the most amazing stories I've run across in my whole life." A big smile filled his face. "I do believe none of you would take the time or the effort to concoct and perpetrate such a hoax. Therefore, THIS is totally amazing. Totally amazing."

Ralph looked at Margaret and Fred. "What's your schedule like next Monday or Tuesday with visitors?"

Fred chuckled. "One moment. Let me make a quick call." He walked outside and was soon back again. "We have no scheduled visitors at all on Monday."

Ralph gave a big smile. "Let me call the station. I'd like very much to sit down and interview all of you, regarding the story. Is it possible for all of you to meet here next Monday morning?"

Everyone shook their heads in the affirmative.

Ralph continued. "I've never come across anything, so incredibly impossible and yet… here it is. This story will make an absolutely terrific hour special. We'll take everything back to the station and do our editing. We might even get to air in a few weeks." He raised his right hand up, pointing with his finger. "Maybe." He smiled.

"I want to thank all of you for your time this morning. I'll see you all back here on Monday morning. Is nine good for everyone? It'll give me time to do a little research before I do my interviews." Ralph turned to Bob. "I really do appreciate you telling me about this. I truly believe this is going to turn into a very special story." He looked at everyone there. "Monday morning. Nine." A big smile filled his face.

Ralph and his cameraman turned and left. Bob accompanied them to the truck to see them off. The rest of us went and sat down at the table.

Bob came back with a big smile on his face and sat down. "I hope everybody's happy. This could be a big deal. Ralph was telling me. After he shares his story this evening on the news, it's likely due to its bizarre and unusual subject matter, the national networks will get wind of it. And of course, it'll most likely be in the Yahoo news clips on the Yahoo homepage. Some of the still photos his cameraman took today he's going to make available to anyone who wants them. So, heads up. Your smiling faces may be plastered across the news and the internet."

Margaret clapped her hands together. "This is so exciting. I can't believe it's actually happening. And Fred, think of the publicity for the Studio. It's wonderful."

I looked at Brandon. "Craziness like this for me is really not a problem. I'm only a short-order cook, artist and writer. But for you. What could this do to your career?"

Brandon laughed. "Hey. It might make me famous. I might even make more money than I'm making right now." He flexed his eyebrows and continued to laugh.

Bob gave a sigh. "Well, I have to admit. This has been a very interesting morning. What can I say?"

Brandon smiled at everyone. "If it's possible, I'd like all of you to join me for lunch."

Margaret spoke up. "Brandon. Thank you so much but Fred and I need to head back to Portland and the museum."

"Well, I want you both to arrange it with the main office in Portland, so you can join me for lunch next Monday after the interviews." Brandon then turned to Bob. "I hope you can join me for lunch today. I'm taking Boo and he's not about to tell me 'no'." He again looked over at me and flexed his eyebrows with a big grin.

"Brandon, I'd love to. And by the way, I know a great seafood restaurant if you're interested."

Brandon smiled. "Then, I'll follow you in my car."

We helped Fred load the table, chairs and his coffee maker in his SUV then all said our goodbyes with hugs and indicated we'd see each other on Monday. Brandon, Bob and I headed to our cars. Next stop was the restaurant.

When we all arrived and headed in, Brandon commented he was very familiar with the restaurant and its excellent food and service but he hadn't had the chance to eat there yet.

After eating and having our last cocktail, Brandon turned to Bob. "Would you mind terribly if I stole your house guest for the rest of the day? I'd very much like to talk with him."

Bob gave a big grin. "Something tells me the both of you have a huge amount of things to talk about and it can't possibly be done by the rest of the day. If it works out and I'm sure it will, I don't expect him home until you both have covered all the subjects I'm sure will come up." Bob looked at me with a huge smile. "I'll see you when I see you. I'm going to call the office and let them in on what's going on so I don't get fired." He started laughing out loud.

All we could do was join in the laughter.

CHAPTER XIII

Walking into Brandon's house, I was amazed at how beautiful it was.

Brandon looked at me. "It's a three-bedroom house and if you like, you have your choice of any of them." He gave a big smile and flexed his eyebrows. "I'm going to fix something to drink. I saw what you had at lunch. Would you like one of those?"

I turned to Brandon and smiled. "That would be perfect." I went and sat down on the sofa in his living room while he went to make cocktails.

"Brandon, please don't think me nosy but you seem to have done very well."

Brandon called out from the kitchen. "Not to brag but in the office in the basement, you can see several awards I've been given for excellence. Yeah. God and the Fates have been kind to me. I've done quite well."

Returning to the living room, he handed me my cocktail and sat in a chair across from the sofa. "You know. Bob was absolutely correct. There's so much I want to say and talk about, I hardly know where to begin. This whole thing is so weird and bizarre. Who'd have ever guessed?"

I shook my head. "You sure as hell have that right." I took a sip of my drink. "Brandon, this is very good. Thank you."

Soon, we began talking about the dreams. We also began to realize how much we were like the individuals in the dreams. Brandon was no longer a fisherman and I was no longer some golden-spooned rich kid from Boston but it didn't seem to matter. Our inner personalities seemed to be the same.

"Boo. I loved you so much. I felt an incredible connection with you." He looked down into his drink for a moment then looked at me. "I'm almost afraid to tell you this because it's so strange. But I feel that same strong connection with you right now as I felt back then."

I was flustered. I took a sip of my drink. "Brandon. Oh, my God. I thought it was just me. I, too, feel that same connection with you. How can this be possible? We really know nothing about one another."

Brandon shook his head. "Something tells me the dreams and the Fates have drawn us together. I believe Richie and Farin wanted us to meet. I think we already know enough about one another. The rest is just small stuff."

I looked hard at Brandon. "Brandon! Look at you! Do you realize how handsome you are?" I turned my head, looking around the entire room. "And look at this place! It shows you're either extremely successful or..." I bent my head down and started giggling. "Or extremely in debt."

My comment made us both laugh.

I continued. "A man like you could have anyone he wanted. Now, look at me. I'm a short bald guy who's a short-order cook, making just enough money to pay all his bills and put a little away for a rainy day." I took another sip of my drink. "This isn't the nineteenth century where the pickings were slim and you had to settle for what you could get."

Brandon looked hard at me. "What are you talking about? Let me explain something about Farin. He knew of others in his world. But they were not the ones he wanted. They were not the ones he had a connection with. Boo was exactly what he was looking for. He liked everything about Boo, physically and otherwise. He loved your personality, your humor, the man you were inside. And whether you believe it or not, I feel exactly the same way about you. I look at you and I go crazy inside. Physically, you're exactly what I've been looking for. And as far as your economic status is concerned, that's of no consequence to me. The love I had for you back then has spilled over into my life, now. I feel exactly the same toward you now as I did then. You know. When I was swept overboard and knew it was my ending, I had one last moment of joy before I died when I cried out. 'Boo, I love you. I love you, silly goose. I'll love you forever.'"

There was a long period of silence before either of us spoke.

I finally broke the silence, speaking softly. "Brandon, you're correct. The same love I had for Farin has spilled over into the love I'm feeling for you. It's just I can't imagine a handsome successful man like yourself, having feelings for someone like me."

Brandon shook his head. "You do realize, I'd love to come over there and just shake you. You have the audacity to conjure in your mind the kind of man I should be seeking. But it's ME who knows what I want. What you think it is, is totally incorrect, you silly goose." He stood up. "Now, come over here, so I can hug you."

I set my drink down on the coaster and walked over to Brandon. We hugged each other. I could feel it. It was exactly the same. It was like it was meant to be. In my head, I could hear Dionne Warwick singing. 'Feeling old feelings again.'

After a few moments, Brandon pulled away and looked at me. He spoke softly. "Now, do you understand?"

I chuckled and shook my head. "Yes. Yes, I do."

"Okay. Let's go sit in the den. The news should be coming on in a little while. I'm really interested in seeing what Ralph has to say. After the news, I'll fix us something to eat. Let me have your drink. I'll freshen it a bit."

I handed Brandon my drink, grabbed the coaster off the table and headed into the den.

Brandon called out. "I'll be there in just a few and turn on the TV."

Within a little while, the six o'clock news came on. We sat there, anxiously wondering what Ralph was going to say. Eventually, his smiling face appeared on the screen.

"Good evening, ladies and gentlemen. I'm Ralph Aker and I'm going to tell you a story you will not believe."

For the next almost eight minutes, Ralph hit intriguing highlights of the story as still shots filled the screen. I have to admit. His choice of comments, regarding the dream segments, definitely left you wanting to hear more.

"And so, ladies and gentlemen, the total story is one which will truly amaze you. In the weeks to come, I'm going to do a special to cover this whole story in detail. It will include interviews with all who were involved and the special will take place at the Winslow Homer Studio in Prouts Neck, Maine. Until then… goodnight."

Brandon continued to stare at the TV. "Wow. He truly is a good reporter. In just a few minutes, he really got across what he had to get across. He did an amazing job. It made you want to hear the whole story. We'll have to find out when it's going to be on and watch it."

"Brandon." I chuckled. "I'll most likely be back in Atlanta."

"Back in Atlanta? The only reason you're going to be back in Atlanta is to tie up loose ends there. If you'll consent to it, I want you to come back here, live with me and stay with me. I lost you over a hundred years ago. I'm not about to lose you again."

I was totally bowled over by Brandon's comment. So matter of fact. So bold. So right out there. No wonder he did so well in his field of finance. He was a man who could take command. "Oh, wow. Brandon, I love you so much, how can I possibly say 'no'? Do you realize every time I see you or think about you, I hear the words of the Elton John song? 'You're all I ever needed. Baby. You're the one.'"

We stood and hugged each.

CHAPTER XIV

Bob was ecstatic when the next day, he heard the news about me and Brandon. He was very happy for me. We three went out to dinner that night to celebrate. The moving transition from Bob's house to Brandon's was quite easy. Bob was really happy because now he had one more special friend.

Before Monday rolled around, I began to hear from folks in emails, texts and phone calls. All were regarding the Winslow Homer dreams. It seems Ralph's report had gone viral on the internet. The Yahoo homepage had several news clips with photographs all taken from Ralph's report.

Joe, the waiter from work, shared several texts with me, saying he was looking forward to hearing a lot more about the story. He was also extremely impressed with Brandon who happened to be Farin in the Winslow Homer time. The same was true for Michael in Richmond, Rick and Julian in New York and Eric and Sam in Boston. All were tremendously happy Brandon and I had found one another and I was moving in with him in Portland. They all asked me to send them a copy of Ralph's report when it was aired if it stayed local.

* * * * *

We all gathered at the Studio early that Monday. Fred even brought in another bigger coffee maker to make sure there was enough for everyone. Shortly thereafter, Ralph and his crew arrived. He very much wanted to set up lighting and cameras in the room where the paintings were located. Margaret and Fred indicated it wasn't a problem.

We all pitched in, moving furniture around while Ralph and his crew set up the lighting and camera stand. We went out front and had coffee while Ralph and his crew did their testing to make sure all was in order. When they were finished, they joined us and had coffee.

Ralph looked at everyone and smiled. "I hope everyone's ready. Before I do any interviews, I'm going in and do some preliminary camera work on the letters, photographs and paintings. When I have all that done, that's when I'll start the interviews. And by the way, if you'd try to keep it down. Even with you sitting out here with the doors closed, the microphones pick up every sound."

Ralph and his camera crew finished up their coffee and went into the room to do what they needed to do. It was about twenty minutes later when Ralph came out front where we all were sitting.

Ralph grinned. "Okay. This is going to be the order of the interviews. First, it will be Fred. Then Margaret. Then Brandon." He looked at me and chuckled. "And last but not least… Guess who?" He then turned to Bob. "Sorry, Bob. Hate it for you but you're left out of this one." He paused for a moment. "You know what? WRONG! Bob, I want to interview you first."

Everyone was surprised.

Bob looked at Ralph. "Really?"

"Yep! You bet. Look. If not for us being friends, I might not have had the chance to be the one doing this amazing story. So. Yes. You really are part of the story as well."

We all looked at Bob and smiled. A huge smile filled Bob's face. "Hey. You never know." He flexed his eyebrows. "Some guy out there might see me and call me up for a date."

I yelled out. "YeeeHaw!"

We all smiled, laughing, cheering and clapping our hands.

Ralph continued. "Do remember. Just because your interview is over, doesn't necessarily mean it's over. Something may come up in another interview, requiring me to talk with you again. So. Is everybody ready?"

We all looked at one another and started laughing.

Ralph looked at Bob. "Okay! You're up!" He then looked at Fred. "Fred! You're up next!" Ralph and Bob left to go in.

We all sat rather quietly, mumbling a little bit among ourselves. Shortly, we saw Bob return. He looked at Fred. "Your turn." He smiled.

Fred got up and went in.

We all looked at Bob. "What did he ask you?"

"Just stuff about how he and I met, what I do for a living and how I found out about this story. Not much else."

After a while, Fred returned.

Fred looked at Margaret and smiled. "You're up." Margaret got up and headed in.

Brandon, Bob and I turned to Fred. Bob asked. "What did he want to know from you, Fred?"

"He asked about the acquisition of this property by the Portland Museum and its restoration as well as some of its history and some of what I knew about Winslow Homer."

Not long afterward, Margaret returned with a smile on her face. "That wasn't so bad after all." She looked at Brandon. "It's your turn."

Brandon got up from his chair and looked at everyone. "Wish me luck." He gave a 'thumbs-up' with his right hand.

I turned to Margaret. "Margaret. What did Ralph want to know from you?"

"He wanted to know some interesting details about Winslow Homer and his history. He also wanted to know about the letters, the paintings and the photographs. I told him all had been authenticated for that time. Except for the new portrait. I'm sure he'll probably do some further research, especially on the photographs to prove they're genuine."

We sat there, drinking coffee and just chilling out for almost an hour. That's when Brandon returned and sat down.

Brandon shook his head. "Wow. Ralph really knows his profession. He's an excellent interviewer. He knows just the questions to ask to eliminate the deadwood and how to make sure he has the whole story." He looked at me and smiled. "Okay, Boo. Now, it's your turn."

Everyone looked at me and chuckled.

I went in and sat in the chair. Ralph stood up and looked at me from all directions. Momentarily, his right hand went up to his chin and he smiled. "Visually, everything is just perfect. I was a little afraid there might be some light, reflecting off your head but everything's fine."

I laughed. "Geez. I guess you're right. Didn't think about the chrome-dome here."

We all laughed.

He wanted me to start from the very beginning and not leave out one piece of information or detail. I indicated to do so would take a chunk of time. He chuckled. "That's why they invented editing."

That made everyone present laugh again.

I told the story in detail. But when I got to the part of hearing about Farin's death, memories returned and I started getting emotional. Tears began running down my face and I turned and looked at the portraits. "We were so happy. Everything was going our way. Hearing he was dead was devastating. I loved him so much and couldn't imagine life without him."

I bent my head down sobbing. "Ralph. I'm so sorry but it's so real to me in my head. And the pain. I can feel it as if it were yesterday. I'm sorry."

Ralph spoke quietly. "Not to worry. Your expression of emotion only proves the intense love you both shared. I got a similar reaction from Brandon as Farin was drowning at sea."

Momentarily, I composed myself and continued. "So, I wrote the letter to Uncle Winslow and walked into the sea. It wasn't fair.

It just wasn't fair." After a short pause, I continued with the rest of the story to the end. "They smiled at me, turned and walked into the light. They're together and their love continues even beyond death."

Ralph smiled. "Thank you ever so much for sharing that. I tell you now. This story is going to make an incredible special. I just hope I can fit it within the allotted time."

I walked out front and smiled when I saw everyone. They all smiled back but then got very strange looks on their faces.

Brandon's mouth twisted. "Your eyes are red. What's wrong? You've been crying."

I shook my head and bent it down. "I swear every time I get to remembering about Farin dying, it gets all over me. Those same emotions from back then rise up in me as if it just happened."

Brandon got up, walked over and hugged me.

I pulled back, looked up into Brandon's face and smiled. "You do realize if not for them, you and I may never have met. You're correct. The Fates work in mysterious ways."

Ralph walked out of the Studio. "I want to thank you all so very much for cooperating and giving such excellent interviews. Because they were so thorough, I need nothing more. I gratefully appreciate it. The guys and I need to head back to the station and get some work done. One last thing before we go. I'd like to get a video shot of all five of you here in front of the Studio. Stay seated. That will be perfect."

Brandon turned to Ralph. "I was so hoping you and your crew would join us for lunch."

Ralph smiled. "Brandon. Thank you for your kindness and consideration but seriously, we have a ton of work to do. Would it be possible to take a rain check?" He gave a big grin.

Brandon smiled. "You've got it!" He gave Ralph a 'thumbs-up' with his right hand and they bumped fists.

As the camera was rolling, we all were smiles, waving and laughing.

Ralph clapped his hands together. "Perfect! Excellent!"

Brandon stood up, smiled and stretched out his right hand. Ralph reached out and shook Brandon's hand. At that, we all stood and he shook everyone's hand. He turned to Bob. "Stay in touch. Don't be a stranger. And thank you ever so much for letting me in on this story. I owe you one."

Bob smiled. "You're so welcome. You owe me nothing. That's what friends are for."

*   *   *   *   *

Over the next two months, I went back to Atlanta and got all my ducks in a row there. Everyone was so happy for me and wished me well. I told Brandon we could put much of my stuff in storage until I could sort it out. I also began looking for a position as a short-order cook. I told Brandon I wanted to try and at least share some of the finances. I wasn't about to have him pay for everything. And any money I had leftover, well, we knew who was going to invest it for me.

We kept watching and watching to see about Ralph's special report but there was nothing. Maybe it had been nixed by the owners of the station and network. Strangely enough, it was the very next week when the station began to place periodic ads, regarding the special. It was finally going to be shown. What was really amazing is the special was going to be shown on the national network as well and would be an hour and a half long.

We contacted Bob, Margaret and Fred and asked them over for dinner and drinks the night of the special. We thought it would be so neat to have everyone there together, watching the show. We were so pleased when all agreed.

When all had arrived at the house, Bob indicated he'd spoken to Ralph. "He told me it was going to be not only about the dream but also some historical information on Winslow Homer. He hoped we all liked it."

After dinner, we all sat down in the den and readied for it to begin at eight o'clock. Everyone got comfortable. It finally started.

"Good evening, ladies and gentlemen. This is Ralph Aker and I'm going to tell you a story tonight that's going to be totally unbelievable and impossible. And it may never have happened if not for a very good friend of mine who led me to it. You'll meet him shortly. We have hired actors to play the roles in this dramatization of the events of the story. Not to worry. You're definitely going to meet all the real people actually involved. When all is said and done, I believe you will understand. Truly, the Fates work in mysterious ways."

"So, I tell you now. Put all your skepticism and your typical logical thinking away. For the next hour and a half, what I ask is you open your mind to the possibilities. I give you fair warning. This story contains very adult subject matter and would not be suitable for children. It would also not be suitable for ignorant, intolerant and bigoted people. And you know who you are." Ralph gave a big grin.

We all looked at one another and broke out laughing. We quickly hushed as the special continued.

"I have titled this program. Two Portraits in Oil. I did it for good reason. It deals with the story, surrounding a pair of oil paintings done out of an incredible love, joining lives from one century to another and even into the beyond. You'll understand totally when this has concluded. During the program, you'll be seeing pictures of paintings, letters and photographs. They will enhance and help you understand more clearly." He smiled. "And now. Two Portraits in Oil."

The program began, interviewing Bob. Next, Fred and Margaret with some history of Winslow Homer and his move to Prouts Neck, Maine in eighteen eighty-three. Paintings done by Winslow Homer.

Then the dramatization began. All was acted by actors playing the roles. It was like watching a movie of the entire event from beginning to the end. It began with Richie, the eighteen-year-old rich boy from Boston going to Prouts Neck. The story continued with the time Farin at age forty came back into the picture, continuing all the way to Farin and Richie, together, walking into the light at the end.

It then continued with interviews with Brandon and me as well as the paintings from the collection, the letters and the photographs. There was more of me talking about the portrait I painted. Also Brandon's and my present lives and work. Margaret's interview made comments about the letters and the photographs as well as the original paintings and portrait as to their authenticity.

The final interview was with Fred who explained the renovation and restoration of the Winslow Homer Studio, its hours of operation and where people could donate to support and maintain the Studio. The last few moments of the program was of all of us out in front of the Studio, smiling, waving and laughing.

Then, Ralph gave his final commentary. "Ladies and gentlemen. I must tell you. When I first got wind of this story from Bob, I was extremely skeptical but curious. It sounded so outlandish and impossible I had to check it out. Now. You've heard and seen the story, the interviews, paintings, letters and photographs. Whether or not you believe it is totally up to you. It's your choice. If I didn't think it had credence, I'd never have done the story."

"I've always heard we have dreams for many reasons. Some are obvious both medically and scientifically. But then there are the reasons beyond the edge. Some say they're predictions of the future. Some say they're warnings and omens. Others say they're ways the dead can communicate with the living. Whatever the reasons, tonight you've heard a very interesting and rather baffling story, regarding dreams and their ties to reality."

"Personally, I not only believe these sequences of dreams were so the dead could communicate with the living but so the Fates could bring two individuals together in this time. Yes. Believe it or not, the two men involved with the dream sequences are now a couple. Because of the dreams and the circumstances surrounding them, they got to meet and got to know one another. They're even talking about marriage, should it ever become legal. I wish them much joy and happiness. And it was all because of some dreams. If not for the dreams, they most likely would never have met. It also shows love transcends death and continues into the beyond."

"Now. Many of you may be totally disgusted and offended this is the story of a love between men. Well. That's your problem. I told you in the very beginning, it wouldn't be suitable for you but you didn't listen. And why does it disgust and offend you? Their love and the idea of two of them getting married doesn't affect you, so why are you so agitated by it? Do you sit and imagine two men together sexually? If you do, you're a sick individual and you need help. What they do in the privacy of their own dwelling is NONE of your business and doesn't affect you in the slightest. So. Get over it."

"Your narrow-mindedness is a disgrace to society and humanity. Slowly, you ignorant, intolerant and bigoted people will drop dead. And what will be amazing? They'll only have to bury your bodies because your heads have been buried in the dirt of ignorance your whole lives." Ralph smiled and paused, thinking there might be a chuckle or two.

His comment had us roaring with laughter. But we quickly got quiet to hear the remainder of his commentary.

"Yes. You'll be gone and the continued rhetoric of discrimination and hate, using religion as a weapon, will diminish as well. And good riddance to you all. The world will be a better and more wonderful place without you."

"This is the twenty-first century, not the nineteenth. The wheels of progress are moving slowly forward and are going to leave those of you in the dust who are ignorant of the true, legitimate modern knowledge and who are intolerant in your thinking. As the Bob Dylan song goes. 'Oh. The times they are a-changin'.' And thank God they are."

"I'm curious how many of you are running to your phones right now to call the station to tell them to fire me." Ralph shook his head and laughed. "Well, let me tell you. I wasn't sure if this station and its affiliates would allow this story to be told due to its rather controversial subject matter." He got a big smile on his face. "But. Guess what? I went and presented it to them, hoping they'd consider it and allow me a one-hour special. I was extremely pleased. The owners and upper management felt it was an amazing and incredible story and should be aired. They all agreed since the story was so involved and intricate, it needed at least one and a half hours of airtime. I personally applauded their open-mindedness and modern thinking. My hat is off to all of them. So, you can forget suggesting I get fired. Cause it ain't happening, Baby. Intelligence and understanding have won out again over your stupidity, ignorance, intolerance and bigotry. Get it?" A giant grin filled his face.

"So. Ladies and gentlemen, I want to thank you very much for joining us tonight and watching. This is Ralph Aker, signing off. And as the great and legendary Paul Harvey used to say at the end of every one of his programs. 'And now you know… the rest of the story. Good day.'" The screen faded and went to a commercial.

We all immediately stood up, jumping around, hooping, hollering, clapping and hugging one another at how terrific the program was. Bob said he'd call Ralph the next day and tell him how much we enjoyed it.

*   *   *   *   *

Bob did call Ralph. He told us the station had received a huge volume of calls applauding it for doing the story. We also told him we were all so amazed at how closely the actors chosen to play the parts looked so much like us. Ralph was super pleased.

Not long afterward, I was contacted by several art galleries in New York who had seen Ralph's report and pictures of my work on the show. They were wanting to display my work for sale. They were extremely pleased with their quality and excellence. They also wanted to sell my novel, regarding the whole event when it was completed and in print.

Brandon was so happy for me. He had a feeling with the amount of work I was going to get, painting for the galleries, I wouldn't have to worry about doing short-order cooking any longer.

Fred and Margaret wanted my book to put on display and for sale when it was finished. It would so enhance the collection. I definitely had my work cut out for me. The front cover was a no-brainer. It would be a picture of the portrait.

*   *   *   *   *

Little did everyone know and much to their amazement, the Supreme Court legalized same-sex marriage the very next year in June of two thousand and fifteen. Brandon and I were ecstatic.

We planned our wedding for June of two thousand and sixteen. Needless to say, we got permission to hold it on the grounds of the Winslow Homer Studio with the ocean as a backdrop. It seemed the fitting place where two centuries of love were finally joined and we toasted to forever.

And wouldn't you know it? Bob was right. Believe it or not, because of the report, he did meet someone and they started dating. I was so happy for him. Bob's a good man and deserved to have that kind of happiness.

We were so fortunate all our friends were able to come. Everyone was so taken with the whole story, they said they weren't about to miss the culmination of it all. Even Ralph came with his camera crew to use on his six o'clock news segment. Margaret and Fred indicated they wanted a photo of Brandon and me from our wedding to put with the collection at the Studio.

While Ralph and his cameraman were filming, I happened to glance up onto the balcony of the Studio. I was shocked. I nudged Brandon, Bob and Ralph. I spoke quietly. "Look. On the balcony. Do you see what I see?"

Unconsciously, the cameraman turned in the direction of the balcony, filming.

Brandon spoke quietly. "I don't believe it. Can it possibly be true?"

Ralph whispered. "Tony. Keep filming and don't stop. Oh, my God. This is amazing. If it comes out on camera, this is going to knock some socks off. Trust me. Wow."

Everyone at the occasion, seeing us looking up, did the same. There was a gasp and low muttering.

On the balcony, were two smiling figures, standing slightly in the shadows, looking down at Brandon and me. They finally realized Brandon and I had seen them when we both raised the glasses we were holding in their direction and smiled. Tony was getting it all on film. They both slowly bowed their heads in the affirmative several times, continuing to smile. Then, they just slowly, slowly vanished into thin air, right before everyone's eyes.

At that moment, everyone went crazy. Their comments filled the air.

Ralph turned to his cameraman. "Tony. I know you had to have gotten all that. Please, roll it back and check?"

Tony reversed the video then ran it, so Ralph could see. Ralph gasped. "Oh, my God! There they are! Clear as day! And Tony had zoomed in on their faces. You can see them so clearly. Look at those smiles. It's as if they came to give their blessings on this wedding. How amazing is this? And look. There they go. Fading. Fading. Fading. Gone. Wow. When management at the station sees this, they may have me do another follow-up special. Yeah."

Bob looked at Ralph and laughed. "I have a feeling you're totally correct."

I looked at Brandon. "I have a feeling Ralph is right. They came to wish us well. They want us to share the love they never had the chance to have here in this life. To me, it proves, even more, you and I are meant to be together." I looked up into Brandon's wonderful crystal blue eyes. "Brandon. I love you so much."

Brandon smiled. "Boo. I love you so much, too, silly goose." He pulled me to him, we hugged tightly and he kissed me.

Everyone watched, smiled and clapped their hands. Cheers rose from the guests.

I knew my life was going to be one many could only wish for. I was loved by an incredible individual just as I loved him.

Yes. I had virtually finished writing the story but this would be the final touch to end it. It would be my next book. I'll have to come up with a good title. Hopefully, the one I want to use hasn't been used by someone else already. Yeah. I must admit. I really liked the title Ralph used for his special. Maybe he'll let me use it. Two Portraits in Oil. I really liked that.

Oh. And just so you'll know. I did NOT wear a wig, wedding dress and veil. Geez. Give me a break.

So. Again. Just as the great Paul Harvey used to say at the end of his radio shows. "And now you know… the rest of the story. Good day."

The End